A
Harlequin
Romance

*Matthew fran abel
1972*

STAFF NURSE SALLY

by

MARJORIE NORRELL

HARLEQUIN BOOKS

TORONTO
WINNIPEG

First published in 1965 by Mills & Boon Limited,
50 Grafton Way, Fitzroy Square, London, England,
under the title "There's Always Someone".

© Mills & Boon 1965

Harlequin edition published
July, 1965

Reprinted 1972

Printed in Canada

CHAPTER ONE

"You got a late pass for tonight, Sally?" Betty Maxwell looked up and studied her finger-nails, which she had just so carefully varnished, but Sally was outlining her pretty mouth with lipstick and did not answer for a moment.

"No," she managed at length. "I've had one, and I'm not at all sure Sister Trask would approve of a second one within the week . . . not as we're so short-staffed and all that sort of thing. Besides, Mike won't want me with him tonight. He's trying to get an interview with young Lord What's-it who's coming to open the new ten-pin bowling alley. He'll be 'on the job', and to a born newspaper man —and that's what Mike is, even if he does work in a small provincial town like Barcaster—the job's the only important thing when he's working. A story's a story," she laughed, mimicking the young reporter with whom she went around so much, but her laughter was tender and kind.

Betty, satisfied now that the varnish was dry, stood up and looked thoughtfully at her room companion.

"Why don't you marry him, Sally?" she asked quietly. "The poor boy's obviously dying to ask you . . . why don't you give him a bit of encouragement and put him out of his misery?"

"He *has* asked me . . . four times," Sally told her, suddenly serious, "and if I thought going around with me was making him miserable I'd end it here and now. But he doesn't want that," she went on. "He says he would rather carry on as we are, rather special kind of good friends, than be without me, unless there's someone else I . . . fall for," she ended lamely.

"And there isn't?" Betty was quick to take her up on the point as she hesitated.

"No . . . o," Sally said slowly, shaking her head of softly waving chestnut-brown hair from her face and turning back to the mirror. "If there was, you'd be the first to know, Betty. You know that, don't you?"

"I thought I would," Betty said shortly, "now I'm not so sure. For all I know, you might be like the majority of the nurses here at the General and be carrying a torch for Curtis Palmer."

"And what if I am?" Sally whirled round from the mirror, her sherry-brown eyes glowing suddenly in her small, vivid, heart-shaped face. "He's the most wonderful man I've ever met," she said slowly and with deep sincerity. "A wonderful surgeon, an understanding man, a marvellous doctor . . ."

"Spare me, spare me!" Betty laughed, shaking her short, soot-black curls until they danced and laughter bubbled in the depths of her long, slanting green eyes. "I know all the rest. I ought to, I've heard it so often from all the girls. But *you* . . . of all people!"

"Oh, I'm not *mooning*." There was scorn in the last word. "I know there's nothing in it for me. Curtis will have to find someone special, when he does settle down— if he ever does—but he doesn't appear to know women exist except in two states, nurses and patients. Apart from that they're obviously just a series of bodies, a series of 'the most marvellous machinery ever known'," she quoted Sister Tutor with a laugh, "all in need of his attention or helping him in the process of giving that attention. They just don't exist otherwise."

"Then why," Betty asked patiently, "carry a torch? If you quite realise it's a waste of time and emotion, why do it? Why not settle for Mike Amberton, who's got where he is by sheer hard work and enterprise and will probably become an editor before very long, adore you, provide you with a comfortable home and take care of you . . ."

"Because," Sally picked up her coat and prepared to leave the room the two shared, "I don't want a passive existence. It wouldn't be fair to marry Mike, feeling the way I do. Marriage without love always seems to me to be a kind of cheating. I know it's done, perhaps more often than we realise. Some girls marry to get away from home. They could just as well take a job some place else and try standing on their own feet for a while. Some girls marry because the man who asks them is the man some-one else wants . . . and no more reason than that. Some marry for security, some for the children they hope will be the result of a marriage, others for the sake of a home of their own—no one else to tell them what to do, or so they think. There must be thousands of reasons why people marry, but to my mind," she was suddenly more serious than usual, "it's wrong to marry without love . . . without the other person being the one who matters more than anyone else in the world, more than family, more than parents, more than the children to come . . . that's the only reason, in my opinion, for a true marriage. And that's why it wouldn't be fair to marry Mike, no matter how many times he asked me, because, fond of him as I am, I could never feel that way about him, and he doesn't deserve anything less."

"After which long speech"—Betty, too, made a grab for her coat, collected handbag and gloves in one fell swoop and took a last, quick glance at herself in the mirror—"you'll miss your bus into Barcaster unless we step on it. We've an awful lot of stairs to descend, remember."

"You'll miss it too," Sally observed. "Come along."

"I'm not coming into town today," Betty volunteered the information as they pelted—as nearly as they could without running the risk of encountering objecting authority—downstairs and out of the nurses' home. "Pete Bradley is taking me to Lyndover. We're going to watch some gliding—he's fascinated by it at the moment—and then have tea at the club-house, coming into Barcaster for a late supper at the Green Bay Tree. What about you?"

"Mike's covering the Spring Flower Show," Sally said, looking anxiously down the road to try and discover whether or not the bus had gone. "I love spring flowers, so I said I'd go along for the ride. I expect we'll do a film, if he has time before whatever else his editor has put on his slate for today. Then I might walk back along the river road . . . it's such a lovely evening, and if Mike comes back with me he'll probably miss his interview with the ten-pin man, and then he'd be in trouble."

"There's Pete, on the corner," Betty interrupted, waving at the angular-looking young man who sat at the wheel of a small, rather battered sports car which had once been white. "Shall I get him to turn around and give you a lift into Barcaster first? It won't make much difference to us . . . and I can't see that it matters, missing one 'tow off' or whatever they call it."

"No, thanks. The bus is coming now. I can see it rounding the bend." Sally craned her neck, turning suddenly back to her friend as, with a rakish swerve, the white sports car came towards where they were standing at the kerb. "Betty," she said in a quieter tone, but suddenly anxious, "watch your step. Pete's a grand chap, but he's out for a good time and for what he can get. There's more than one nurse at the General has cause to wish she hadn't ever gone around with him for a spell. It always seems to end in heartache, but not for him."

"I can cope," Betty returned confidently. "I like men with a bit of 'go', but I don't let 'em break my heart.—It's made of that new plastic stuff, you know, the kind that bends but doesn't break, always comes back to its original shape."

She waved cheerfully as she swung herself into the seat beside the driver, but before Sally could return Pete's salute the huge crimson bus lumbered up and she was being urged by the conductor to: "Hurry along there, please." She climbed up to the top deck, intending to enjoy a quiet cigarette during the ten minutes or more it took the bus to reach the town, and smiled to herself as she turned round and saw the little white car just disappearing from view, going in the opposite direction.

Sally lit her cigarette and relaxed in the wide seat, thinking over the conversation she had just had with Betty. Betty had been her close friend now for more years than she could remember. They had been friends at school, been parted when Sally went to the local Technical College *en route* for enlistment for her nursing career, and Betty, determined to shake off what she called 'this urge to slavery', had taken a one-year course as a shorthand typist.

It hadn't worked, and eventually they had started together as student nurses at the Barcaster General Infirmary. Their progress had been steady and satisfactory, but not spectacular, and now, Sally reflected proudly, they were both staff nurses at the Barcaster and the next step would be towards Ward Sister. She sighed. She had spoken the truth when she told Betty she would never marry for any reason other than love, but a career, however satisfying, could never take the place of the dream of her heart, a happy home life with the man of her dreams, the man almost every other girl at the hospital idolised in some way or another, Curtis Palmer, the brilliant and handsome young surgeon who did not seem to know that the other sex existed in the way of companions, sweethearts or wives.

'He must have had a mother,' Sally reflected, still thinking of him as she often did when she was alone, 'whether she's still living or not. Maybe he has sisters . . . if he has they didn't do a very good job of putting him at ease with other girls.'

Her thoughts flew to Michael Amberton, the young journalist who had started as a cub reporter with the *Barcaster Chronicle* about the same time as Sally had begun her career at the infirmary. They had met at a hospital ball, where Mike had been sent to 'cover', and it had been Sally who had put him right with what he termed "the names and the definitions of the bigwigs". She had liked him at once. In some ways he reminded her of her brother, Paul, and Mike had been ready to be liked by anyone, especially a pretty young nurse.

Sally valued their friendship, and knew she would have felt lost without it, but not for the first time she wondered now if she were being unfair to go around with Mike when she knew she could never love him and he, it was obvious, had thoughts in another direction entirely.

'We'll see,' Sally told herself philosophically, rising and making her way down the swaying stairs as the bus neared the Town Hall, where the show was to be held and where Mike would be waiting for her. 'I'd hate not to go out with him again . . . we enjoy ourselves so much, except when Mike gets . . . silly ideas.'

Mike was standing on the steps of the Town Hall as the bus pulled up, and came running down to meet her as he watched her descend the steps.

"Thought you'd missed the bus," he began, taking her by the arm. "It must be running late. There's only two minutes before the Mayor's car's due to arrive and the Mayoress opens the show."

Still talking, he piloted her to the place he had selected as being certain of giving her a good view of the proceedings and the opportunity to hear all that was said, then, with a murmured excuse, he was gone.

Sally was not disturbed. She had attended many functions in Mike's company and knew now what to expect. He had his report to write up, and he was keen on his job. She was quite content to look about her, to admire the flowers, inhale their heady perfume and to see who else was present. The Spring Flower Show at Barcaster was an annual and traditional event, and Sally always enjoyed coming to it. One day, she vowed to herself now, when she was no longer a career girl but had a home of her own and the time to spend on things like flower growing and arrangement, she, too, would proudly bring her entry and, she assured herself, not worry as to whether or not it won an award so long as it was considered worthy of exhibition!

She was roused from these day-dreams by the uncomfortable feeling that someone was staring intently at her. She swung round, expecting to see one or other of her nursing friends, but to her amazement she found herself staring almost directly into the eyes of Curtis Palmer. For a moment Sally was swept off her guard and the ready colour rushed into her cheeks, making her annoyed and strangely embarrassed. After all, why should she not come to the show if she wanted to?

"Don't look so guilty, Nurse Nesbitt," Curtis spoke in a low, controlled voice, but Sally could hear every word.

"I know it's your free time! Tell me," he went on, "are you here just as a spectator or because one of your own efforts is to be judged . . . or rather has been judged?"

"I . . . just as a spectator," Sally managed awkwardly. "I came with a friend. We generally come to things like this . . . he's a newspaper man . . . but," she added for no apparent reason, "I love the show itself . . . so much colour and perfume, and the promise of so much more to come . . ."

"Yes," he agreed quietly. "That's the wonderful thing about this show in the last week of April, there's all the promise of the summer ahead . . . if we have any summer this year!" He smiled suddenly, making himself look years younger, almost boyish. "I came because my mother's tulips have been awarded a medal," he confided. "It means so much to her if someone else in the family comes too . . . but I can't stay very long."

He glanced anxiously at his watch, and Sally guessed he must be due in the theatre again that afternoon, but there was no time to make further comment, for the Mayoress was now advancing, carrying the bouquet of spring flowers which had been presented to her on arrival.

Sally watched and listened intently, enjoying every moment. She was thrilled to hear the Mayoress comment on the "beautiful parrot tulips, with their wonderful blaze of colour, grown by Mrs. Curtis Anderby Palmer . . .", but she did not turn round to look at Curtis, knowing instinctively that it would embarrass him if she did, but some instinct told her also that he would be pleased she had been present to hear his mother's effort commended.

At last the Mayoress ended her speech and the show was declared open to view so that those present were free to wander round and to comment and admire and to make up their minds which exhibits they would bid for when the auction of the exhibits (for charitable purposes) took place in three days' time, when the show was ended.

Mike was by her side all the time, taking notes on the speech and more short notes as he examined the prize-

winning efforts, but when the Mayoress had declared the
exhibition open and she was free to move around with
everyone else Sally looked for Curtis Palmer. He was
nowhere to be seen.

They stayed at the exhibition until Sally had had her
fill of the sights and scents of spring, and even a slight
headache from the concentrated perfume in the air, then
Mike announced he had one more "job" to do before they
could have tea. The job, this time, was not of long
duration. It consisted of collecting from a colleague notes
on the conclusion of a case in the magistrate's court which
Mike had covered so far, but which had unfortunately
been carried on into the afternoon.

"Now," he announced once he had his data and his
friend had bidden them a cheery 'so long', "let's go and
eat. I'm starving. Didn't have time for lunch. Shall we try
the Copper Bowl, or would you rather go Chinese?"

"The Copper Bowl, I think," Sally told him. "I like
the atmosphere there. We can talk, too."

"And that's enough for you, isn't it, Sally?" Mike
looked down at her slight, small figure beside his own. He
would have given a great deal to have been able to introduce her to his friend as 'my fiancée', but he knew Sally
just wasn't interested. All the same, Mike possessed a
natural aptitude for looking on the bright side of things
and firmly believed in the old adage, "If at first you don't
succeed, try, try again." He tried again now. "Don't you
think it would be grand if we could go . . . *home*, together, for tea?" he asked. "I'd work like a beaver if I
knew you were there, waiting for me . . ."

Sally looked up at him, liking his frank grey eyes, his
unruly dark brown hair, the broad shoulders and the
height of him and the general feeling of reliability he
always gave her, but not, she told herself firmly, not
loving him . . . not as she knew she would love the man
she eventually married.

"You couldn't work any harder if you tried," she commented briefly and truly. "You work all hours as it is. No,
Mike," her tone softened, was tender as it always was with
him, working some unconscious magic in his heart as it

always did, quite without Sally's being conscious of doing so, "I've told you before . . . four times now"—her eyes widened reproachfully—"and you just won't believe me. I couldn't *like* you better than I do, I couldn't depend on you, trust you more, and I love being in your company, but I just don't love you . . . not in that way . . ."

"I don't believe it," Mike's wide mouth set stubbornly, but there was a twinkle in his eyes. "You just don't want to admit it," he observed, "or else you don't know love when you meet it. It'll come, I'm not in any hurry. When you've had enough of this career business I'll still be waiting, and if"—he shrugged his broad shoulders philosophically—"you find someone you *do* love, or think you love in the meantime, well, we'll have all this to remember"—he gestured dramatically. "And now"—the grin was back—"since you won't let me propose to you again let's go and eat. My working day's not half over yet."

The Copper Bowl was a favourite meeting and eating place of theirs, and the waitress who had come to know them hurried forward, anticipating their order. When she was out with Mike, Sally always chose what she termed "man-type meals", and today was no exception. They decided together, and had generous helpings of steak, fresh salad and fried potatoes, followed by apple charlotte and cream, then, for Mike, the coffee for which the Copper Bowl was justly famous, and, for Sally, a pot of tea, which she loved. They talked of all manner of things over their meal, but although he said nothing else of an intimate nature, Sally knew how Mike's thoughts were running, and when he offered to drive her back to the nurses' home before going on to his interview she protested, quietly but firmly.

"I'm going to walk back by the river," she told him. "You get off and interview your bowling man. I want to think."

Mike protested, but he knew he had a job to do and that Martin Howbury, his editor, would expect him to do it well. There was no need to worry, he told himself. Sally had walked back along the river road hundreds of times before, both with him and alone or with some of her nurse friends, but for some reason, tonight, he did not want her to go.

"Let me get you a taxi," he suggested. "Or," as he saw her look of protest, "at least put you on the bus." But Sally was adamant, and at last, still wishing he could have delegated the job of interviewing the man coming to open the bowling alley to someone else, he watched her until she was out of sight, then, with one last wave before she rounded the bend, he turned the little car and headed for the centre of the town.

Sally walked along, sauntering rather than walking. She wanted to think, to be alone for a little while, away even from Mike's solicitous care of her and from Betty's loving, friendly chatter. The river road was, as almost always at this time, nearly deserted. One or two couples walked slowly along, their arms entwined, taking no notice of either Sally or anyone else but each other. She walked until where, standing by the low wall which guarded the unwary child from falling into the swiftly flowing River Barr, she could look up and down stream, almost to the hospital on the one hand and down to the high bridge which opened to allow the occasional sea-going boat to pass through.

For a time she stood there, just gazing, lost in thought, then her attention was caught and held by a movement on the bridge itself. Sally held her breath. Someone else was dreaming too, and in a very precarious position. Unless she was extremely lucky there could be a serious accident.

CHAPTER TWO

SALLY drew in her breath and tried to strain her eyes to see more clearly just what was happening. Apparently nothing at all was happening. There was undoubtedly a girl sitting on the parapet, as lost in her thoughts as Sally had been in her own, but she wasn't moving, wasn't, it seemed, even aware of her surroundings.

Sally thought quickly. 'Nobody can know she's there,' she reasoned to herself. 'It's the most deserted part of the river road now. There's hardly anyone comes along here since the new road went through and up-town. She must have wanted to get away from everybody . . . to think something out, maybe. But whoever she is, she ought not to be perched up there. It may be all right now, but once she tries to move she'll likely lose her balance . . .'

Making up her mind on the instant, she turned and began to walk as quickly as she could in the direction of the bridge. The pathway along the river road was uneven and hard to the feet, but Sally pressed on. The girl sitting easily on the parapet did not seem in the least disturbed by her position. She had made no movement at all since Sally had first caught sight of her, so it was quite evident she had not gone there with the intention of jumping off or anything of such a dramatic nature.

All the same, uneasy without knowing why, Sally hurried along, covering the short distance back along towards the bridge at a far faster rate than she had walked before in her life, and all the time she kept her gaze fixed on the figure of the girl. She was thinking as she hurried, and all at once it struck her that she was being unusually presumptuous in assuming that anything *could* be wrong. Certainly the girl appeared lost in thought, and in addition, Sally decided, studying the slight figure above, her whole attitude was one of utter dejection. But to assume anything wrong on such slight evidence savoured suddenly of cheek . . . interference.

'She probably has a perfectly good reason for sitting up there,' Sally told herself, but reason intervened, telling her that no one would choose such a dangerous position if they had ever really stopped to think about what they were doing.

'I could be meandering back to the home and thinking quiet, serene thoughts about Curtis Palmer,' Sally argued with herself. 'At least I know now that he *has* a mother, and that she likes flowers . . . that's more than I knew about him when I left the General this afternoon.' But she knew she could not turn round and go back without first having made at least an attempt to find out whether or not everything *was* all right with the girl on the bridge.

'If I went up the steps and on to the road,' Sally reasoned to herself, passing one of the steep flights of stone steps which led up to the new by-pass, 'I could talk to her then.'

She swung off in her tracks, making for the steps, and was happy to see some signs of life now she was nearing the town. A familiar big red bus lumbered across the roadway above her. Two cars and a shooting-brake followed. There was a small café ahead too. It was there, obviously, for the convenience of long-distance travellers, but Sally had the sudden thought that a cup of strong tea would be more than welcome at this moment. There were other signs of her nearing approach to town. A telephone kiosk, a bungalow, way back off the road and surrounded by a formal garden, but Sally's attention was abruptly diverted from looking about her. She halted, halfway up the steps, as, apparently deciding to retreat, the girl on the parapet began to move.

Even from where she stood Sally felt she could sense the indecision which attacked the other as soon as she made the first move towards return. The slight figure tensed, seemed to crouch against the parapet as though hugging the brickwork, seeking contact with something solid. Then, as the girl obviously gathered her wits together and, presumably, summoned up her courage, her foot slipped, and the event which Sally had been anticipating and almost unconsciously preparing for actually happened. There was a shrill cry which sounded thinly on the evening air, then, with a wild flailing of arms and legs, the figure of the girl hurtled from the high parapet towards the swirling waters below.

Sally was never sure, afterwards, whether she really heard the harsh, cracking slap when the girl's back hit the water, or whether she had only imagined it, but what she did remember was thinking that with an impact like that it was quite likely the girl had broken her spine.

She did not pause to think or to reason. She turned and raced back down the steps, pulling off her coat as she ran. She tossed it on to the bank, covering her handbag, kicked off her shoes and left them there, wincing as she climbed the low wall bordering the path and stubbing her toes as she did so. The girl was floating, face uppermost, coming towards her on the strong current, and Sally breathed a prayer of thankfulness that it was so, for the Barr was a tidal river and at times the current was very strong.

Thankful now for all the swimming lessons her brother had given her, and for Paul's insistence that she should continue with her practice until she had achieved her life-saver's badge and her gold medal, Sally struck out, con-serving her strength for the task which lay ahead, for the figure being brought towards her. She reached the girl fairly quickly, but she was apparently unconscious.

'At least she won't struggle and make things difficult,' Sally comforted herself as she slipped her hands under the girl's armpits, turned on her back and struck out for the shore.

It was hard going, for with the coming of evening the wind had freshened and the current seemed determined to take the girl along with it on its way out to the North Sea, but Sally was equally determined and hung on grimly, forcing herself to keep a steady rhythm and pray-ing desperately someone would come along and see what was happening. Nobody *did* come along, and once she reached the bank it took all Sally's remaining strength to drag the girl clear of the water and to lay her just beneath the wall on the narrow strip of ground which bordered the river itself.

The girl *was* unconscious, but, Sally was thankful to note, she was still breathing. There was a dreadful stillness about her, however, which, to Sally's trained eye, spoke of something more serious than a mere loss of conscious-ness and of having had the breath knocked out of her by her impact with the water.

'She could have fractured her head, her spine . . . any-thing could have happened after an impact like that,' Sally thought, listening for the girl's heartbeat, which was so faint as to be almost imperceptible. 'I've got to get help . . . and quickly.'

Wincing for her own toes, she scrambled over the wall again and picked up her coat, returning with it to cover the still figure, then she was back over the wall, her shoes on, her handbag in her hand, heading for the telephone kiosk she had noticed but a few minutes before.

She had never in her life been so pleased to hear any-one's voice as she was to hear that of Kay Lawson answering from the switchboard at the General. In a few moments Sally had told her all the necessary details and been assured an ambulance would be along from the hospital in a matter of minutes.

"Watch yourself, Sally," Kay added in friendly tones before she rang off. "April is no time to be taking a plunge into cold water! Keep moving while the ambulance gets there. I'll see they hurry even more than usual."

Thankfully Sally hung up and hurried back to where she had left the girl. Help was coming, and it could not get here too soon. She was thankful that the girl had not, apparently, swallowed much water—that, she told herself, would be because she had hit the water on her back—but if her charge's breathing had been faint at first it was even fainter now, and Sally bent anxiously over her, doing what she could but restricted by the knowledge that there might be serious internal injuries and that, without medical help, she might be doing all the wrong things.

She slapped her own thighs and arms, trying to restore the circulation, for although she had been helped by her brisk trot to and from the telephone kiosk, she was, by this time, shivering and her teeth chattering. It was with a tremendous sense of relief that she saw the ambulance coming over the bridge. It was moving slowly, and Sally knew the men would have a hard task to spot her in the rapidly dimming light. Desperately she took off what had been a crisp white blouse when she had started out that afternoon and, standing on the edge of the bank so that she would be outlined against the background of the water and the evening sky, she flapped it frantically, fearful that she could not be seen. After a moment or two spent in crawling slowly along the road she saw the vehicle halt. The headlights flashed once, twice, and Sally knew she was being signalled, she had been seen. Again she made the effort to scramble over the wall and went running to the foot of the steps to meet the two men who were coming down towards her, carrying a stretcher.

"Here," she gasped, still shivering. "On the other side of the wall. I couldn't lift her over."

"Put this on, Nurse." One of the men, the elder, stripped off his coat and handed it to her. "You climb aboard," he added in kindly tones. "We'll cope from now on."

"I think she's badly injured." Sally knew they both knew their job as well as she knew hers, but somehow felt she had to let them know of that awful impact on the hard surface of the water. "I heard the way she hit the river," she ended, her voice tailing off.

"She'll be injured all right," the man said. "Lucky she isn't dead, jumping from up there . . ."

"She didn't," Sally protested. "Jump, I mean. She was . . . just sitting there when I first saw her. She tried to get back and she slipped."

"Takes all sorts to make a world," the ambulance man observed. "I could think of better—and safer—places to ruminate if I had to. Still, none of us knows what makes the others tick. Come on, Bill, you take her feet."

Sally scrambled back over the wall yet again, hugging the thick coat round her. She poked her chilled feet back into her shoes, which she had slipped off again when she had reclimbed the wall, then, picking up her handbag, she began, wearily, to climb the stone steps which led back to the roadway. By the time she had pulled herself aboard the ambulance she felt as tired as if she had been on nights, and without adequate rest, for a month.

It seemed ages before the men returned, carrying their burden carefully on the stretcher. The elder of the two men peered closely at Sally before he let in the clutch.

"You all right, Nurse?" he asked quietly. "You'd better get some attention yourself as soon as we're back at the General. We'll take the young lady into Casualty and you can give whoever wants it your version of what happened when you've taken care of yourself. Don't want you down with pneumonia, now, do we?" he added with a laugh.

"I'll report to Sister Trask," Sally said quietly. "She's Duty Sister, and," she went on with a rueful smile, "I can't think what she'll say to me, coming back to the hospital in *this* state!"

"A great deal less than she'd have said if you'd stood by and watched the girl drown," the ambulance driver asserted. "Always one for duty, is Sister Trask. She'll say you did the right thing, but she'll expect you to have the sense to take care of yourself as well. And I've no doubt you'll do just that," he ended, adding as the ambulance rolled smoothly down the hospital driveway: "Here we are. You drop off here, Nurse. We'll look after your patient. No need to worry. Everything's under control."

Sally thanked them, offered the driver his coat back, only to be told briefly to "keep it on, love, and keep out the cold," then she hurried indoors in search of Sister Trask as fast as she could go. Sister Trask's comments were brief and to the point. She listened intently to Sally's account of what had happened, nodding but not saying anything until the girl's quickly-told story was ended, then she gave the brief smile which always surprised Sally by the way in which it lighted up the severe, controlled features.

"You did very well, Nurse," she said quietly. "Very commendable. I'm proud of you. And now, run along and get a hot bath—as hot as you can bear it—and I'll have someone bring you a drink which I'll mix myself. Then straight into bed with you, and we'll have a full report of this in the morning."

Sally was only too glad to hurry along as she had been bidden. The chill which had wrapped itself about her when she emerged from the river seemed by this time to have penetrated into her very bones. She ran her bath of very hot water as she had been instructed and, on impulse, added a handful of the pine bath crystals Betty had given to her some time previously. Then she shed her wet things and submerged, allowing the warmth and comfort of the water to seep into her chilled limbs.

She was roused from a semi-stuporous condition, induced by the heat of the water, the fragrance of the pine bath salts and sheer physical exhaustion, by the sound of hammering on the door of the bathroom and Betty's demanding voice.

"Are you all right?" she was saying. "You've been in there ages, and here's me with a witch's brew from Sister Trask which she said I'd to see you drank while it was nice and hot."

"Coming!" Sally called back, rousing herself and climbing out of the now rapidly cooling water. "Just a sec!"

She dried hastily, pulled on her pyjamas and dressing-gown, which she had brought in with her, and opened the door.

"I think I'll have that in bed," she announced, indicating the covered beaker Betty carried on the little tray. "I'm tired out."

"Not to be wondered at, either," Betty scolded. "I can't let you out on your own a minute but what you find some lame dog or other to rescue. I take it this was after you left Mike?"

"On my way back to the nurses' home," Sally said briefly, snatching up her clothes and towels. "Come on. If you have a minute I'll tell you what I can . . then I'm for bed."

"Me too, as soon as I've reported you're O.K.," Betty told her. "Sister's worried about you. Says it must have been a strain getting that girl to the bank and then on the shore all by yourself. What really happened?" she ended, opening the door of their joint room and carrying on the conversation as if the question had never been asked. "I put the fire on. Thought you'd not want to come into a cold room, and it soon cools off once we've switched off and got into bed."

"Thanks." Sally pulled one of the two small armchairs up to the little one-bar fire which the girls used on especially cold days or nights to augment the central heating which did not appear to function quite so well in the nurses' home as it did in the hospital itself. "It was like this," she began, and, taking the hot drink from her friend, grimacing a little at the taste as she took an experimental sip, she launched into her story.

"She *didn't* jump," she said, as she reached that part of the story, "though why she went up there in the first place if she didn't expect to slip, I can't imagine, but anyway I'd gamble she was as surprised as anyone could be when her foot slipped as she tried to get back and she found she couldn't make it."

"Must have given you an awful shock," Betty prompted with genuine understanding and sympathy. "What did you do first?"

"I tore back down the steps as fast as I could make it, pulling off my coat on the way," Sally recited slowly as she relived the scene over in her mind. "I don't know what else," she ended lamely. "I . . . just sort of jumped into the water and struck out for her."

"Rather you than me," Betty shuddered. "Was she unconscious?"

"Yes, but breathing. I was thankful enough for *that*. I think she must have injured herself—the impact, you know—so I was glad I didn't have to apply artificial respiration and all that sort of thing. As it was, I covered her with my coat and then hared off for the telephone kiosk as fast as I could make it. The rest you more or less know."

"I wonder who she is?" Betty speculated. "Slater put her to bed, and she says her clothes were all the very expensive ones, not the sort of things you buy off the peg. Hand-made undies and all that sort of thing. Must be someone with money."

"I've seen her somewhere before," Sally mused aloud. "I can't quite remember where, but it was probably at one of the functions Mike's covered from time to time. She drives a bright red sports car around, an expensive-looking thing it is too. She's evidently local."

"If you weren't so worn out, and I know you must be," Betty admitted, "I'd suggest going down to the telephone and giving Mike a ring. He'd be sure to know who she was if you described her."

"And be sure to make a paragraph at least out of it for the *Chronicle* when it comes out on Thursday," Sally added promptly. "No, Betty. Much as I like Mike and much as I know what his job means to him, this is one occasion where I'm not going to have him making something out of nothing. Not that he does," she amended hastily, "but you know what I mean. Whatever the reason she had for sitting up there in that dangerous and precarious position, whoever she is, she was obviously wanting to be alone . . . didn't want to share her broodings with anyone, whatever they were about. She had the misfortune to slip . . . I had the fortune to save her life. The least I can do is to keep quiet about it, until I know whether she wants her—stupidity publicising or not."

"Maybe you're right," Betty sighed, "but I'm afraid my natural curiosity would get the better of me if I'd had the adventure and the star reporter of the local rag was my current boy-friend."

"Which he isn't," Sally put in smartly, ignoring Betty's disbelieving giggle. "Friend if you like, but not a *boy*-friend, not a special friend."

"Anyhow," Betty smothered a yawn and rose, "whoever she is, she owes her life to you, and let's hope she realises that. If you've finished with that beaker now I'll take it down to the kitchen and report to Sister Trask that you've suffered no ill-effects so far. She'll want to know all about this in the morning——"

She broke off as a knock sounded on the door and, opening it, she found the rosy face of one of the ward maids confronting her.

"Matron says she is very sorry to disturb you if you have already retired," she said plainly and distinctly, "but if it is possible she would like Nurse Nesbitt to come to her office for a few moments. The mother of the girl the ambulance brought in a little while ago would like to speak with her."

CHAPTER THREE

"Gosh!" Betty ejaculated, as she closed the door after taking the message. "She must be somebody important . . . Matron would never have disturbed you tonight if she hadn't been. She's too thoughtful for that. Feel up to it, love?"

"I shall have to feel up to it, as you put it," Sally said in a resigned tone. "Besides," she admitted with a slight smile, "I must admit to more than a small share of that curiosity of yours, though I wouldn't have done anything personally to satisfy it, not like ringing Mike, as an instance. This," she conceded, "is somehow different."

"Something like the mountain coming to Mahomet instead of his going to the mountain. I see what you mean." Betty was already pulling out a clean uniform for her friend. "You'll have to go looking your beautiful best," she said, laughing. "Can't let the old firm down. By the way, what was she like? The girl in the river, I mean."

"Horribly wet," Sally laughed, "but I know what you mean," she added hurriedly, as she caught her friend's indignant glance. "Well, let me see. I couldn't have told from the way she looked this evening, but I know I've seen her somewhere before, and her hair is long and fine, beautifully done as a rule, and, as the old fairy tales used to have it, it looks like spun gold when the sun shines on it. She's small, delicate-looking. I don't know, but I bet she'll have those big, wide-open specially melting type blue eyes. She certainly has the longest lashes I've seen on anyone, and they weren't false either." She was dressing rapidly as she spoke and paused now to apply the light touch of make-up permissible in the hospital. "By the way," she turned round, a twinkle in her eyes, "did you remember to take the varnish off your nails this time?"

"Yes, I did," Betty grinned, as they both recalled the last occasion she had 'dressed up smart' because Pete liked his women that way, and had not had time to take off the forbidden varnish before it was spotted by Sister Trask. "I learned my lesson," she announced ruefully. "I carry a bottle of varnish remover now . . . one day it'll break and spoil my handbag, but even that would be better than facing Sister without remembering to take it off."

"It's the rules," Sally said, scarcely listening, then, turning round, "will I do?" she ended anxiously. "I look sort of . . . drained. Must have been the hot bath or whatever was in that awful concoction Sister sent up for me."

"More than likely to be caused by your icy plunge and your Herculean efforts at rescue," Betty remarked firmly. "You look fine," she continued sincerely. "The typical young staff nurse . . . now be off with you, before my compliments go to your head!"

Laughing, Sally picked up her cloak and put it on, ready to traverse the long drive-way which connected the home with the hospital, and in a few minutes she was tapping quietly on Matron's door. The controlled contralto voice bade her come in, and Sally opened the door, smiled into the eyes of Miss Langley, the youthful Matron of Barcaster General, before becoming really aware of the woman who rose from the low easy-chair in which she had been sitting, to greet her.

"This is Mrs. Bodman, Nurse," Matron performed the introductions from where she sat. "Mrs. Bodman, this is Staff Nurse Nesbitt, the young lady you wished to see for a few minutes." There was no emphasis on the last few words, but Sally had the distinct impression that Matron was indicating that Sally had experienced an exhausting time herself and should not be kept very long. But she knew now why she had been sent for. The girl whose life she had saved was this woman's daughter, and the woman was 'Mrs. Bodman'. The elder Mrs. Bodman had, Sally knew, been dead for some years, so long ago that she did not remember her, but old Sam Bodman, wealthiest and most influential man in Barcaster, was the Chairman of the Hospital Management Committee, and therefore a very important man.

"I'm delighted to meet you, Nurse." Stella Bodman held out her hand to grasp Sally's in a firm grip. Sally found herself looking at the tall, well-made woman who towered over her and instinctively reflecting that whoever else she might resemble, it was certain that little Miss Bodman did not take after her mother. It was only then that she became aware of the man who stood now behind his wife . . . he had been quietly waiting behind her chair, and who now held out *his* hand to grasp Sally's own.

"As Francesca's father, I'm happy to echo my wife's words," he said quietly, and, looking at the tall, lean figure with the scholarly face, the strong depth of character outlined in every feature, Sally reflected that Francesca—since that was obviously the girl's name—did not resemble her father either. Her unspoken query was answered by Robert Bodman a second or so later. "When my father returns," he said, every word distinct and emphatic, "he will not be able to do enough to show his gratitude. He adores Francesca," he smiled, and Sally was surprised at the difference this made to his stern face. "She is the image of my mother, you see," he ended, thereby in some strange way settling a strange disquiet which had been present in Sally's mind ever since she had discovered that the rather severe-looking couple before her were the girl's parents. "He will want to see you," he ended gently, "just as we did . . . to thank you."

"I—it was only what anyone else would have done," Sally said sincerely. "It just so happened that I was the only person there, so it had to be me or . . ." she finished, aware the sentence was wrong, but too embarrassed to care.

"Well, thank God you *were* there," Robert observed. "And that you kept your head and acted so promptly and efficiently."

"Was there anyone with her, Nurse?" Stella Bodman's steel-grey eyes seemed to probe into the depths of Sally's mind as though in that way she could be certain of the truth. "Anyone in the car . . . on the bridge?"

"I didn't see the car," Sally said truthfully, "and certainly there was no one on the bridge."

"Whatever possessed her to do such a thing," Stella went on, "we can't imagine. But once she's well enough I must get to the bottom of this. There's a reason somewhere."

"She slipped, you know," Sally said quietly, aware of Matron's watchful gaze. "She was sitting there ... I saw her a long time before she tried to come down. It looked as though she wanted to sit and think, where she wouldn't be disturbed," she said haltingly. "I don't know, of course, but that's how it looked."

"She has her own room at home," Stella said crisply. "She could have gone in there to ... think, if that was what she wanted. But she hasn't been at all like herself for a few months now. I wonder," she whirled round suddenly and smiled at Matron, "is it too much to ask if Nurse—Nesbitt, did you say?—could sort of look after Francesca in a somehow *personal* way? I don't know what your term is for it, but do you know what I mean, Matron? Sort of a special nurse on Francie's case ... at least for a time. I like you"—she turned back unexpectedly to the girl. "There's such a trustworthy air about you, and Francie will be grateful, I know, when she hears what you did. If you could gain her confidence, let me know where we have gone wrong," she went on in an almost pitifully pleading tone, "we might be able to have a little more understanding—something like Grandfather has for her—next time she has problems to solve and he isn't here."

"Miss Bodman will certainly require what we term 'specialling' for a few days, anyhow," Matron conceded. "I don't think there is any reason why Nurse Nesbitt should not undertake her case. I think it may help in recovery," she smiled.

"Matron—I—will you tell me how she is now, please?" Sally asked. "She was so still ..."

"She is still being examined," Matron said quietly. "She has been X-rayed, of course. There is a slight fracture of the skull, nothing much to worry about, it seems, and the spine is contused. So far she isn't very aware of her surroundings." She smiled at the girl and nodded her dismissal. "You will be able to see her in the morning," she announced, "and by that time, after a good night's rest and sleep, she may be able to manage a word or two. We'll see."

Sally thanked her, said goodnight to Francie's parents, and made her way back to the nurses' home, thinking about the lovely girl whose life she had undoubtedly saved.

'Obviously money isn't everything,' Sally told herself with an inward smile. 'I'd rather be me, worrying about my tired feet and aching legs and whether I can make my pennies last out until next pay-day, than be someone like Francie, with the sort of problems that make her choose such a dangerous place to . . . think.'

She pulled her cloak more closely round her as she prepared to leave the shelter of the corridor for the walk along the drive-way which linked the nurses' home to the hospital itself. She was tired, and she ached in every limb. 'Unaccustomed exercise,' she told herself firmly, but she felt strangely happier now about the girl whose life she had saved.

"Hasn't anyone told you that you ought to be in bed, Nurse?"

Sally came to herself with a start as she suddenly found the tall, bulky figure of Curtis Palmer blocking her way. In the light from the corridor his fair hair appeared to have a nimbus round it, and she stood for a moment, blinking up at him, to find the blue-grey eyes with their faint shadows under them watching her with unmistakable concern.

"What are you doing here?" he demanded. "I've been examining Miss Bodman and I heard all about what you had done. She may be slim and slight, but she can't have been an easy burden . . . and she was wet through . . . so must you have been." He appeared to be making conversation, Sally thought stupidly, as though anxious to talk, although why she could not imagine. "I should have thought Sister would have sent you to bed," he continued, almost in a grumbling tone.

"She did," Sally hastened to say. "I've had a . . . concoction Sister Trask mixed herself. I've had a hot bath, and I was just about to climb into bed when Matron sent for me because Miss Bodman's parents were here. They wanted to see me."

"So I should imagine," Curtis said briefly. "I know you couldn't very well refuse, and Matron would feel she had to send for you, but I think you should pop off now and climb into bed as fast as you can. You mustn't be down with pneumonia and unable to go out with your friend on your next free afternoon, now, must you?" he ended, startling Sally by this reference to her excursion earlier that day. "I'd like to say, Nurse," he added, as she murmured her 'goodnight' and turned away, "I think it was a wonderful thing for you to do. Some girls might have lost their heads, run for help, which would have arrived too late, stood there wringing their hands . . . anything but the obvious thing, which you did at no small risk to yourself. The current is quite strong there. You might have been carried down to Wentfair lock or even, eventually, out to sea yourself. Very commendable."

"Thank you, sir," Sally said in a small voice, then, as he turned and hurried on his way down the corridor, she pulled her cloak around her once more and set off down the path, her heart unaccountably singing.

She was dying to talk to someone about it. Curtis Palmer, the surgeon all the nurses raved about—or almost all of them—had stopped and expressed his concern about her welfare, had praised her actions, which had been reported to him—probably by the ambulance men—which had saved Francie Bodman's life. She was spilling over with excitement as she opened the door of the bedroom she and Betty shared, then she stopped, a little smile springing to her lips as she carefully closed the door. Betty lay, fast asleep, in her own bed, oblivious of Sally, of Curtis Palmer or anyone else. Quietly, carefully, Sally slipped out of her things and changed into her pyjamas and slipped into bed.

'Never mind,' she consoled herself philosophically, 'I'll tell her all about it in the morning,' and, smothering a yawn, she fell asleep almost at once.

Morning, however, brought its usual scramble to wash, dress and be down on time for breakfast, and once seated at the table with the others it did not seem the right moment to launch into an account of her meeting with Curtis the previous evening. Several people asked about her adventure, and, mindful that it was very obvious the Bodman family—at least the elder Bodmans—were anxious to avoid gossip and publicity about the incident, Sally chose her words with care, making her escape thankfully at the earliest possible moment to the private ward where Francie Bodman had been taken.

"She's asleep now," Nurse Minden, who had worked in Casualty for the past six months, rose from her chair at the bedside as Sally entered. "She's not really unconscious, more in a state of stupor," she observed. "She keeps mumbling something, but I just can't make out what it is." She handed over Francie's chart as she spoke. "Mr. Curtis will be along to see her later," she informed Sally. "He says she has to have rest and quiet and almost complete isolation."

"In other words, no visitors, unless, maybe, her mother and father for a few minutes." Sally nodded. "That's what I expected. She's lucky not to have a fractured spine in my opinion."

"They're X-raying again, maybe to make sure," Ann Minden informed her. "Mr. Curtis says he wants to be certain. I don't know why they're talking this way. *He's* never uncertain of anything, or doesn't seem to be."

"I expect, like the rest of us, he always likes to make sure," Sally observed. "Thanks a lot, Minden. I'll take over now."

When the other nurse had left she stooped and took a closer look at her charge. Now that the fine hair was dry and had evidently been brushed by someone, Sally realised she had been right in thinking she knew the girl. She was one Sally had seen at several functions which she had attended along with Mike.

'Last time I saw her was at the Press Ball in February,' she remembered. 'She was with her father . . . but I didn't know who they were then.'

The girl on the white pillow stirred slightly and the full, rose-pink lips parted as she whispered softly: "Thirsty . . ."

"Here we are." Deftly Sally slipped her arm beneath the girl's head, supporting her, and with her free hand she held the special drinking cup containing, she knew, a mixture of glucose and water. The girl sipped, pulled a face and turned her head slightly away, and without protest Sally gently laid her head back on the pillow. She thought her patient had relapsed into the almost stupefied condition in which she had found her, but after a moment the huge eyes with their delicately veined lids opened, and Sally found she had been right in her conjecture when she had described the girl to the enquiring Betty. Francie's eyes were large, and almost the exact colour of wild violets, rain-drenched and amazingly appealing. The fabulously long dark lashes fluttered and she spoke again.

"Hello," she said weakly. "Where am I? Nobody has said anything to me . . . not ever since I came here."

"You wouldn't have heard them if they *had* said anything to you, Miss Bodman," Sally informed her quietly. "You . . . had a fall. You fell into the river and I pulled you out. You're in the General Infirmary, and I've been given the job of looking especially after you." She smiled. "I'm Staff Nurse Nesbitt," she added as an afterthought.

"Do I *have* to call you all that?" The big blue eyes were childishly pleading as Francie made an effort to turn her head, but the movement was evidently a painful one, so Sally changed her position so that Francie could see her more easily.

"Not when we're alone," she smiled. "Sister wouldn't like it if we weren't formal, but my name's Sally, and you can call me that if it will make you feel any better."

"And I'm Francie," the girl said slowly. "Francesca, really, but it sounds like somebody else, not me at all. I owe you my life, Sally, don't I?" she went on. "Do you know the old saying—I think it's from the Chinese, but

I'm not sure—that says when anyone saves your life you owe it to them . . . it belongs to them . . . or something," she ended, suddenly becoming confused and unsure of herself.

"It sounds all right," Sally said cheerfully, bending down and smoothing the sheets, placing an experienced hand on the girl's wrist. "But I shouldn't worry about it. I've more than I can do to cope with my own life at times, let alone taking over the management of someone else's! Not to worry about it now. You're to rest and get better," she said with quiet firmness. "We'll talk about it again when you feel a little stronger."

There was silence for a few minutes, then Francie's voice came again, fretful and weak.

"My head hurts and I ache . . . in my back," she said, "but I can't feel my legs. Sally!" Suddenly the weakness in the voice vanished as panic took its place and the blue eyes sought Sally's gaze with their own, seeking reassurance. "*I can't feel my legs,*" she repeated almost shrilly. "They haven't—cut them off, have they?"

"Of course not," Sally soothed her quickly. "They haven't done anything to them. You . . . when you fell you hit the water so hard that you'll have given them a temporary paralysis, that's all. It's nothing to worry about," she insisted, and hoped she was speaking the truth. "All you have to do is to lie here quietly and rest, and allow your body—legs included—to recover from the shock. It will take time, but it will be all right in the end."

"It will? You promise?"

Sally swallowed hard. She was almost sure, but there was always an element of doubt in these cases. So much depended upon the patient herself.

"I'm sure," she said firmly. "You'll soon be as well as ever you were, but you must do as you're told."

"I will," Francie promised, closing her eyes and obviously accepting Sally's statement as the truth. "I'll do exactly as you say. At least I owe you *that* much."

"You don't owe me anything," Sally said firmly, "but you do owe it to yourself and your parents. Now, drink this." She held out the cup again and one of the small white tablets which were to help give Francie the rest her body needed.

Obediently the girl swallowed the tablet, and this time she did not pull a face as she accepted the drink, but as Sally laid her down again she spoke.

"Does . . . Martin know?" she asked in a voice so low that Sally had to stoop to catch the words.

"I don't know who Martin is," she said quickly, "but you can be certain if he is anyone who ought to know what has happened then he will have been informed. And if he hasn't, we'll talk about it again when you wake up, and I'll see what I can do."

The answer appeared to satisfy the girl, for she closed her eyes, and gradually the tablet began to take effect. In a few moments she was sound asleep, and Sally breathed a sigh of relief that her patient had taken the first step on the long road to recovery.

CHAPTER FOUR

As the days slipped by it seemed to Sally that she had always known Francie Bodman, that they had been friends for years. She had seldom felt like this about any-one before, always being a little shy and reserved in the giving of her friendships until she was on what she felt was 'safe' ground emotionally, but with Francie it seemed strangely different.

For one thing, she was so overwhelmingly grateful to Sally for saving her life that it was almost embarrassing at times for the nurse to listen to her. Over and over again, as she grew a little stronger and was able to talk for longer periods at a time, she reiterated the fact that she hadn't meant to fall into the water.

"It must have looked to you—to anyone—as though I'd tried to jump in, to kill myself," she said on the third day. "But I didn't. I can't explain. Mummy asked me this morning what on earth made me go there . . . but I can't make her see. She and Daddy aren't like Grandpa.

B

They can't understand that sometimes I want to be just by myself, not sulking, not talking, maybe not even thinking, though I generally am . . . and they think there's something wrong and come hurrying after me to try and put it right, whatever it is. And most times it isn't anything at all . . ."

"So you went up there to . . . think," Sally said slowly. "Or at any rate, to be alone. Your mother said you have a room of your own. Wouldn't you have been more comfortable there? Or couldn't you have taken the car and driven out to Brockfield Woods or some place where you could have done your thinking in safety?"

"They always find me," Francie said solemnly. "They think it's morbid to want to be alone. They'd like me to have a lot of friends in and around the place. But I don't know many people who like the things I like, and I don't like many of the things most young folks of my age appear to go crazy about. If I go to my room and there's no music coming from the radio or the television, the record player or the tape-recorder, one or the other of them comes to see if I'm all right. If I go for a drive by myself, they offer to come . . . or follow me. Not," she ended quickly, anxious Sally should not get the wrong impression, "because they think I'll do anything *wrong*, but because they want to take care of me, because they're over-anxious about me." She paused for a moment then added softly: "I was a twin, you see. I had a brother, Mark. They thought it was right to let him go ahead, do all the things he wanted to do within reason. They bought him a fast car . . . he wasn't really old enough then. He was killed on our nineteenth birthday, and ever since then they've been afraid to let me do *anything* without one of them, or both of them, being there."

"You poor child," Sally said with true compassion. "So now there's just you . . . and that awful memory every time you have a birthday. No wonder you sometimes want to be alone."

"I have another brother," Francie volunteered. "Alaric. He's much older, though, and he works in some concern of Grandpa's, way down south. I don't know quite what he does, but he and his wife and their two babies come home at Christmas and times like that, but he and Fay have their own lives, their own interests, and I don't really have a great deal in common with either of them . . . not like it was between Mark and me."

"You mustn't brood about it," Sally told her crisply. "You must try to think of the happy times you had together, before the tragedy happened."

"That's what Martin says," Francie said slowly, startling Sally. Francie hadn't mentioned that name since the first day she had spoken to her new friend. "Martin says we must have had some good things to remember, Mark and I, and so we did. He says it's up to me to prove to my parents I'm not likely to—do anything to hurt them. And now," her voice trembled suddenly, "I'm stupid enough to fall off a bridge, and that's all because of Martin, too," she ended, suddenly indignant.

"You mentioned Martin before," Sally said carefully, allowing none of her curiosity to sound in her voice. "I certainly didn't see anyone else with you, so I don't see how he could be the cause of your slipping. I think your foot slipped."

"I wouldn't have gone up there, where I knew I couldn't be seen and where it was very unlikely anyone would think to look for me, if I hadn't wanted somewhere I could be alone and think what was best to do about Martin without somebody asking me what was wrong," she said, obviously believing she had explained.

"I see," Sally said patiently. "But that doesn't tell me very much. Only that you wanted to think about Martin, whoever he is, and that you have to decide some course of action and you don't want any interference."

"I wouldn't mind helpful interference," Francesca surprised her by saying. "But Mummy and Daddy simply wouldn't understand. They'd try to help, and they'd not be able to, and things would be worse than they were before . . . if that's possible," she ended gloomily.

"If I can do anything," Sally suggested rashly, "I'd help, but I'd have to know a little bit more . . ."

"I want to know if he's heard about . . . this." Francie

gestured towards her prone body. "He hears everything. It's his job, so he's bound to know. But what I'm wondering is what does he really think happened? He'd understand . . . he knows how I look for inaccessible places to be alone when anything's bothering me."

"And now he's bothering you, as you put it," Sally observed. "Well, it's my half-day tomorrow, so if you give me some idea of how I may be able to help, I'll have a shot at it."

"I'm sure you could!" Francie's eyes shone and she made a great effort to sit upright, but she was by no means ready for that as yet. She let herself fall back on the narrow white bed, panting from the effort, making no protest when Sally bent and began to take her pulse rate.

"You ought not to allow yourself to get so excited, Francie," the nurse said reprovingly. "If you have a relapse or anything of that sort I may be blamed." She knew she was exaggerating, but it seemed the only way to control this girl who was from such a different world from her own, unused to any restrictions save those imposed by excessive love and protection. "We don't want some other nurse in my place, do we?" she added. "Not when we're just getting to know each other so well."

"Always a good thing, that sort of relationship between nurse and patient, especially in cases of this sort." Both girls looked towards the door, startled, as Curtis Palmer opened it and stood there, his big, bulky frame dominating the small room. "I thought it was time I looked in on you for today, Miss Francie." He smiled at the girl. "How are you feeling now, my dear?"

"A wee bit better, I think," Francie said cautiously. "My head doesn't hurt quite so much, and whatever this is they've given me to lie on, it's helping my back a great deal. But," the plaintive, worried note was back in her voice again, "I still can't move my legs."

"It will take time." Curtis seated himself at the bedside and took the delicate wrist in his strong fingers, checking the pulse rate. Apparently satisfied, he leaned back, smiling gently at the girl in the bed.

"You mustn't worry," he told her, kindly but firmly.

"Worrying would be the worst possible thing for you. You're a very lucky girl—thanks to Nurse here—and in another month or two you'll find that when the physio people have taken over some of your time you'll soon learn to walk again."

"Another *month*!" Francie couldn't have sounded more appalled if he had suggested she would remain in bed for life. "I can't just lie here so long!"

"I'm afraid you've little alternative." Curtis's smile softened as he rose to go, and then he looked directly at Sally. "I'm sure Nurse will take care of you. She must have a personal interest in your case, and there's really not a great deal to worry about now," he added. "Nothing that time and rest won't cure, I'd stake my reputation on that."

He stayed for only a moment longer, commenting to Sally about Francie's remarkable escape, then he left them, but no sooner had the door closed behind him than Francie burst into excited chatter.

"You said it was your afternoon off duty," she began. "Who will be coming in your place? Do you know?"

"Jean Webster," Sally told her. "You'll get on like a house on fire with Jean. She's a friendly girl. Comes from a large family and has a great deal of human sympathy with any problem."

"Well, she needn't worry about mine," Francie said briefly. "I'd rather you helped on that, if you don't mind."

"I said I would help, and so I will," Sally reiterated, "but you'll have to say something more about it. And please be as brief as you can. I'm going off duty in less than half an hour. Jean'll be here then, so if you don't want anyone else to know, start telling me all about it now," she ended, smiling so that the other girl, in her present state, would not imagine she was 'ordering' her to begin.

"There's not much to tell, not really." Francie's eyes held a dreamy expression and her fingers plucked restlessly at the coverlet on the bed. "The whole thing is Martin and his stubborn pride . . ."

"Martin who?" Sally asked with what patience she could muster. She was beginning to think she would have to draw the story from Francie word by word, but when at last the words came she spoke in a breathless sort of rush as though anxious to get it all said and finished with completely.

"Martin Howbury," she spoke the name slowly, carefully, then, as though collecting her thoughts, she rushed on. "He's the editor of the *Chronicle* here in Barcaster. He's good. Grandfather says so, and he ought to know. The *Chronicle* belongs to Grandfather, you know," she added, as though she expected Sally to have the information at her fingertips. "That is, he founded it and he's still the main shareholder and director. Grandfather says Martin will go a long way. He—Grandpa, that is—has interests in two big dailies in London, and he says Martin will make a name there one day. But Martin doesn't want to leave Barcaster. He likes the town and he likes his work, and he's writing another book . . . he's had one published, and he wants to stay here and work on the next and the next . . ."

"Very interesting," Sally commented as the other girl paused for breath, "but where do we go from here?"

"I met Martin because I was in Grandpa's office on the day he came for an interview," Francie went on in the same dreamy tones. "It's some years ago now, so of course I was much younger, but I thought he was marvellous from the very moment I met him. He had so much . . . vitality . . . that's the only word I can think of to describe him. He's so alive himself, so evidently enjoying it all— the job, his work on his books—everything. That's the magnetic part about Martin," she sounded as though she were trying to explain him to herself, "he's so alive, he makes everyone else wish they had the same . . . zest for living. That's how he makes *me* feel," she ended honestly. "I always feel sort of recharged when I've been with him."

"Sounds interesting if somewhat exhausting," Sally commented as Francesca paused again. "But I still don't know what you want me to say to him, ask him or whatever it is."

"Listen," Francesca's tone held the first hint of impatience she had displayed, "it's not so simple as that. We liked each other straight away," she went on. "Grandfather was delighted. He likes all young people, and he likes those who *do* things most of all. He was the one who spoke up for me when Mummy thought I ought not to go to—oh, all sorts of things, the Press Ball, as an instance. Grandpa said it would be good for me to mix with the other young people of the town—all of them, not just those from our own little circle—and he was right. We've had some marvellous times, Martin and me."

"And then?" Sally urged. "Look, I don't want to rush you, but I shall be off in a few minutes."

"Well," Francesca sighed, indicating she was reluctant to cut short what should have been to her a full-length story, "we . . . grew fond of each other. I don't know about Martin, but I think I fell in love with him from the very beginning, and as time went by I thought more and more about him . . . began to dream all those silly little dreams girls are supposed to dream when they . . . fall in love. I thought it was like that for Martin too." Suddenly her voice was softened, made sad by what Sally could only think of as the weight of unshed tears. "I know he loves me . . . in fact he's said he does . . . but . . ."

"But . . ." encouraged Sally, despairingly. "What's the matter? Has he a wife somewhere or other he's collected in one of these bursts of enthusiasm of his?" she ventured.

"Good heavens, no!" Francie was deeply shocked. "He says he's never even had time to fall in love before," she went on earnestly. "He doesn't know much about girls . . . in real life, that is, although"—she gave a restrained little giggle—"I think he does a remarkably good job in portraying them in his books."

"And I've to tell him what?" Sally asked impatiently. "Ask him if he still loves you?"

"I know he does." There was dignity in the few words. "No," she continued slowly, "don't ask him if he still loves me. We'll love each other for always, I know that. But Martin's proud." Her chin tilted a little. "Not with the right kind of pride," she announced. "Instead of being proud that his Maker singled him out—along with a lot of others, I know, but even so he's one of the comparatively few—and gave him a gift, a gift to entertain and to instruct others, a gift of expression, of the use of words such as few people have, he's angry because it hasn't brought him anything like the wealth the varying enterprises of my family have brought to us. But that's not the effort of one man," she went on indignantly. "I know Grandpa's done most of it, but they've all done their share. Do you know," she turned her head to face Sally directly, "that Grandpa has made several fortunes out of all sorts of things, from newspaper companies to holiday camps? He's a finger in all sorts of pies."

"Then he must have what you might call a 'gift' for successful business," Sally observed. "But what——"

"I'm coming to that," Francie cut her short. "I could see Martin was sort of trying to edge me out, make me think he didn't want my company any more, and all the time his eyes told me he was acting a lie. Besides," she added with unconscious self-righteousness, "I know him so well I knew it wasn't the truth. I didn't say anything at first. I let him think I was going along his way, then one afternoon I asked him about it . . . outright. I asked him why he was doing this and—oh, the usual things."

"And what did he say?"

"He said," Francie repeated the words so slowly and so distinctly that Sally knew they must have been alive and repeating themselves in her mind ever since Martin had said them, "that he could never—unless he wrote a best-seller, which he didn't think he ever would—give me the things I'd been used to, the kind of life in which I'd feel happy, accustomed. He said I was to forget about him, ask Grandpa to find 'some other young man more suitable', and—oh, all sorts of things. He said I was to find someone who had more time to play, to take me around, not someone whose nose was to the grindstone of the demands of the paper and his spare time went sitting hunched over a typewriter. He said a lot more," she ended lamely, "and he tried to sound as though he meant it. In the end he went back to the office to finish his leader article and then, he said, he was going home to write the next chapter of his new book."

"Unless he's a very strong-minded or dedicated person I hardly think he'd be doing *that*," Sally observed. "So," she went on, "he went back to the office and you, I take it, went up on to the bridge to think what was best to do next? Why didn't you ask your grandfather to help?" she enquired abruptly. "It sounds to me as though he'd approve."

"He's away until the end of this week," Francie said quietly. "Besides, I know that would make Martin angry. No, I've got to think of a way to make him change his mind all by myself . . . or with your help."

"Mine?" Sally was genuinely startled. "I don't know anything about love," she said quickly, "much less how to cope with a situation like this. What do you want me to do? Go and tell him that you went up on to the parapet to think about what he'd said and were so disturbed you fell in?"

"No," Francie said insistently. "You must know what I mean. People—not all of them reporters—take all sorts of stories to a paper like the *Chronicle*. Someone might have told him . . . about me," she hesitated a moment, then continued, "about what happened, and they might not have told the truth because they didn't know it. To some people it might look as though I went up there to . . . jump in. I'd never have the pluck," she announced. "It's an awfully long drop. I think Martin would know that too," she said soberly, "but he *does* know how Mummy follows me around, wanting to know if I'm all right, if I'm happy, what I'm doing, where I'm going, and he knows I have one or two places—the old apple tree at the bottom of Grandpa's garden for one—where I go to be alone, to think. He'd *know* what happened, if you explained that to him. I just don't want him to think it was . . . anything else."

"I'll go and see him," Sally promised rashly. "A young

man who works on the *Chronicle* is a great friend of mine, Mike Amberton, he'll help."

"Ask him to come and see me, please," Francie pleaded. "Martin, I mean. Your Mike too, if he'd like to, but I *must* see Martin again. You see, one of the last things he said was that we wouldn't meet again only in company. He said he didn't think he could stand it . . . that he didn't want to be alone with me again when he knew it was only fair to say goodbye, and if you could convince him that that would be the most *unfair* thing he's ever done in his life or is likely to do, then I'd be even more grateful to you than I am already."

"I'll try," Sally promised, unable to say any more as Jean walked in at that moment. "I'll pop in and see you before I go up to bed if I have any luck. Now, be a good girl and do as Nurse Webster tells you," she laughed, and to her relief some of the sober concentration left Francie's small face. "See you later," and in a moment or two she was on her way over to the nurses' home to change for her afternoon off.

CHAPTER FIVE

As usual, Mike was waiting for her as the bus drew into Barcaster. His small car was drawn up at the kerb, and his notebook was in his hand as though, even when meeting Sally, he held himself ready to take notes, make comment.

"You look nice enough to eat," he greeted her, his twinkling glance taking in the new leaf-green linen suit, the crisp white blouse with its provocative frilly neckline, the shining hair, brushed to perfection and the small, twinkling shoes. "Much too nice to go milling round a dusty field watching a gymkhana."

"Is that where we're going?" Sally asked with interest. There was one thing about going around with Mike, she did get to so many things she would not have probably even noticed in the local paper, and she could well understand his absorption in his job. There was so much of interest, so much that was different from the ordinary daily round going on all about them, but which, unless one was particularly interested in any one event, one missed, but which Mike covered in his everyday round. "Where is it?" she enquired, settling herself beside him.

"Grayson's meadow. Should be quite a good show. We'll just stay to the end of the pony-jumping contest, then I'll have to be back in town for an hour or so before we can go to the pictures. You did get a late pass this time, didn't you?" he ended anxiously.

"Till ten-thirty," Sally told him, "but I've something to do before then. Mike," she went on in her most wheedling tone, "could you take me to meet your editor when we come back into town, unless *now* would be a more appropriate moment?"

"Now," Mike said firmly, letting in the clutch, "would be a most inconvenient moment, but I have to call in at the office and hand in my stuff for the evening edition when we come back, so I can take you in then. Why?" he demanded curiously. "Don't tell me you have an urge to join the slaves of the pen."

"Nothing like that," Sally assured him briskly. "No, it's a more personal matter. You know I told you about the girl on the bridge when you rang me the other day? She and your editor have . . . I don't know what to call it . . . not an 'understanding', not even that, but she's . . . well, she thinks he and she mean something to each other. She thinks he might have heard something, be thinking what isn't true . . ."

"You mean about her high dive last week?" Mike asked, watching the traffic carefully but taking time to shake his head. "I know there hasn't been anything in the *Chronicle,* either the weekly edition or the evening ones," he assured her. "I kept my word to you and didn't mention it. It seemed important to you that I shouldn't, and you can take that as a very high compliment, since it seems you were the only one who knew anything about it apart from the girl herself, the ambulance men and the hospital authorities. Funny," he went on musingly, "one of the staff reporters usually phones the hospital before going to press each night . . . they usually tell him if there's any out of the ordinary case."

"Not this time," Sally assured him. "The girl in the case happens to be Francesca Bodman . . . you know, her grandfather owns the *Chronicle* and its off-shoots. He seems to be a very important chap one way or another." She paused a moment, then added: "Also he happens to be Chairman of the Hospital Management Committee."

"I know him." Mike gave vent to a low whistle. "I should say they wouldn't want that in the papers. Must have been sheer bad luck it happened, but luck like that doesn't happen to the Bodmans of this world."

"Well, this did," Sally retorted, adding curiously: "What do you mean, Mike . . . luck like that?"

"They usually have all the breaks," Mike said without envy. "Some people are born like that. I don't say they don't work, they do, but so do lots of other people who don't have half the good results the Bodman family have. Old Sam Bodman has only to look at anything to make a mint of money out of it. He's a finger in every pie you can mention. Bus companies, holiday camps, building sites, publishing, the lot. And I'll give him his due, he makes it his business to be no ignoramus on whatever subject he tackles."

"He sounds a remarkable old man," Sally observed. "I don't think I've met him."

"Then that's a treat in store," Mike told her. "He's one of the best, and I mean that. Here we are." He turned off down a side lane already packed with parked cars. "We're going right in," he announced. "Hold tight, it'll be a bit of a rough ride."

It certainly was a bumpy ride over the grass field to the roped-off enclosure labelled 'Car Park', where Mike waved a card indicating he was 'Press' in the face of the man who came forward to charge him a fee, but it was well worth it. The May-day sun shone brightly, and though a chill little breeze sprang up from time to time

Sally wasn't cold. She was enjoying herself hugely, and as she watched Mike's careful taking of notes she wondered how he could always manage to divorce himself so completely from the actual events to give the scrupulously fair and objective reporting of which he was so rightly proud.

They went to the huge canvas tent for a strong cup of tea, served in a thick china mug, loaded with sugar, and ate fat ham sandwiches provided by the local Women's Institute.

"Just the pony-jumping now," Mike consulted his programme, "and then we'll leave. There's not much of interest after that."

The pony-jumping was fun, and Sally fell a complete victim to the charms of a tiny girl very correctly dressed and sitting erect on her mount, two small, stiff pigtails sticking out, one at either side of her small face.

"I hope *she* wins," she whispered to Mike. "Number four, the little girl with the pigtails."

"She will," Mike assured her. "It's a foregone conclusion. Her father's Matt O'Hara . . . trains the show jumpers for Merry's, the soft-drinks people. It's their hobby, the three Merry brothers, and it pays them well. In return they pay Matt well and they're looking after his daughter. She'll end up riding for Britain before she's a great deal older."

Sally watched in great excitement, thrilling as the little girl rode in a triumphant first. She felt as pleased as if the child were known to her personally.

"You're not objective enough," Mike grinned down at her when she remonstrated with him for his lack of enthusiasm. "It *was* a good effort, but I'm here to report the whole event, not just to praise little Miss O'Hara, even though she's done so well. This is a small-town affair, remember, Sally, and a lot of the other kids tried hard too. None of them have the advantages *she* has in training and so forth, but she *will* go a long way," he ended generously. "Now," he tucked her hand under his arm to help her through the crowds, "let's try and get the old jalopy out and head back to town and hand in my report."

"And introduce me to your editor," Sally reminded him. "You did promise."

"For my sins!" Mike grinned again and helped her into the car. "I don't know why you want to see him," he remarked, as he switched on the engine and began to negotiate his way through those who were either already heading for home, for the refreshment tents or for the small fair at the other end of the meadow, "but I hope it isn't for anything likely to upset him. He's a touchy customer, is our Martin. If it's anything about the paper, be careful. He's as full of pride as a monkey is of mischief, and when his pride's touched his temper's uncertain."

"I don't know whether I'll upset him or not," Sally confessed, "but I gave my word, so I'll have to try. Francie—Miss Bodman—wants him to come and see her, and it seems the last thing he said to her was that he wouldn't see her alone again, always their meetings must now be in company."

"He must have a reason." Mike was out of the field now and driving carefully along the rutted lane which led to the main road. "Do you know what it is?"

"Vaguely," Sally confessed, "but this is in confidence, Mike, you understand that?" she added quickly.

"You're the boss," Mike agreed. "Fire away."

"It seems they met when he was appointed editor. She's been about with him on a number of occasions— maybe like I come with you—and they . . . grew fond of each other . . ."

"Like us," Mike put in, and the colour rushed to Sally's cheeks as she protested hotly.

"Not like us," she said indignantly. "Speak for yourself, Mike Amberton."

"As I just said, you're the boss." Mike's grin seemed unshakeable. "I can wait. I'm 'speaking for myself', as you put it, and I'm no weather-cock, but I can wait. Go on with what you were telling me, or we'll be at the office before I know what it's all about."

"Be quiet, then," Sally admonished him. "To continue: Francie is really in love with Martin Howbury. I'm sure there isn't a shadow of doubt about that. She says he has admitted he's in love with her," Sally frowned, trying to remember if those had been exactly Francie's words, but she couldn't, so she let it pass, "but that he says unless he writes a best-seller or something of that sort, he can't offer her the same sort of things and life she's been brought up to. So he thinks they should say goodbye now and she should look for someone else."

"And that's the reason she ended in the river?" Mike whistled softly, and Sally took him up at once.

"Yes, but not in the way *you* are evidently thinking," she told him. "She says her parents are over-protective. I've met them, and I can well imagine. They lost her twin brother a few years ago in a car crash, and that's intensified their care of their daughter. If she goes off on her own for a moment they're after her, wondering where she is, whether there's anything wrong—not spying," Sally emphasised, "but . . . well, trying to make sure she's as safe and as happy as they can make her. Even in her own room in her own home they apparently pop in and out if she goes off on her own to think or anything, so she chose the one place where she couldn't be seen from the road, behind the pillar on the parapet of the bridge, and when she'd done thinking she lost her balance."

"I'm not surprised." Mike pulled the car into the kerb with a flourish outside the building bearing the letters in gold paint over the entire width of its windows 'Barcaster Chronicle and Evening News'. "I couldn't even venture to get out there, let alone sit and think. She must have been pretty desperate in her search for solitude, poor kid."

"That's how I feel about it," Sally said, accepting his hand and descending to the pavement. "She doesn't want Mr. Howbury to think what you thought a few moments ago. She says he'll understand why she had to get to somewhere inaccessible, but she does want him to come and see her."

"Well, try working your undoubted charm on him," Mike suggested. "We're by no means alike, my boss and I, but I've no doubt you can succeed where I'd only be told to mind my own business. This way," he added, holding open the door and leading Sally through the general office to where a door concealed a flight of stairs leading to the office staff's quarters. Mike led the way along a narrow corridor to another door labelled 'Martin Howbury, Editor', tapped lightly and left her with a cheery wave of his hand.

"Wait for me downstairs if you're through first," he suggested. "Or I may have to look in on my way by. If so I'll collect you then."

From within the room a voice bade Sally 'Come in.' It was a deep voice, but brisk, as though its owner had no time to waste on unnecessary wordage. She pushed open the door and found herself at once face to face with a broad-shouldered young man who towered above his desk, looking at her with such bright, interested eyes that Sally thought at once of Francie's word 'vitality'. The eyes were dark brown, so dark as to be almost black, and the thick, dark brown hair on top of the rather narrow high-domed head was as unruly as Mike's always was when he was working on a job.

"Yes?" Martin Howbury began. "What can I do for you?"

"Nothing . . . that is, I don't want you to do anything for me. It's something for a friend of yours . . . I mean that's why I'm here."

One long arm reached out and a faint smile quirked the corners of the full, precise mouth as Martin reached forward a chair and pulled it round to face the desk. Then he picked up a box of cigarettes and proffered it, not speaking until she had allowed him to light one for her.

"You'd better begin at the beginning as Alice or somebody said," he suggested. "First, who are you? And who's this friend of mine on whose behalf you're here?"

"I'm Sally Nesbitt," Sally said briefly. "I'm a staff nurse at the Barcaster General, and a week ago I pulled a friend of yours out of the River Barr."

"Go on," Martin said sharply as Sally hesitated.

"She didn't jump in," she said deliberately, and she

could almost feel him relax and saw some of the acute anxiety leave the bright eyes. "She went on to the parapet of the bridge, to be alone to think. She says you'll understand why she had to find somewhere inaccessible."

"Poor little Francie," the words were low but controlled. "It is Francie you're talking about, isn't it?" he demanded. "Francie Bodman?"

"That's right," Sally said. "I've been looking after her."

"Where is she and, more important, *how* is she?" was the next question. "One can't fall from that height and hit water, water is a hard surface to hit," he informed the girl as though concluding she did not know, "without some damage being done."

"She's been very lucky," Sally told him. "She's badly bruised, naturally, and there was some slight suspected fracture of the spine, but that's not so. She has a contused spine."

"I know, I know," Martin interrupted testily. "I quite understand. Can she walk?" he ended abruptly.

"Not yet," Sally told him honestly. "She'll soon be going over to the physio people for massage and exercise. There's no permanent injury."

"Thank God for that," Martin said devoutly and sincerely. "It would have been awful if—she'd crippled herself. She's so alive . . ."

Sally looked at him in some astonishment, then readjusted her ideas. She had quite seen what Francie had meant when she referred to Martin's vitality, but to think of Francie in anything like the same terms seemed ludicrous, until she reflected that perhaps some of Martin's own vitality and zest for living infected the girl when they were together.

"She asked me to explain all this to you," Sally told him, "in case you'd had a report of any kind handed in and . . . got the wrong idea, and she asked if you would come and see her."

"See her?" The words were shot out as though in response to a command. "I told her I . . ."

"That you wouldn't see her alone again," Sally said

smoothly, as he paused, evidently searching for the right words. "Yes, I know. She told me. But surely . . . the circumstances . . ."

"I can't see what difference the circumstances, as you call them, make," Martin said crisply. "I'm sorry she had this accident. If it makes you any happier I feel a bit guilty. I should have insisted on seeing she went home safely, but I had an urgent job on here, and she said she was going to drive around for a while to think over what I'd said."

"Instead, she went up on the parapet to think," Sally emphasised, "and that's how she came to fall in. I know. I saw the whole thing happen. I can't see," she said almost explosively, forgetting completely that she was resolved to coax him into agreement with her, "what difference coming to see her once would make. She'd know then that you weren't . . . utterly indifferent to what's happened."

"Indifferent?" Martin stood up and if he had towered over the desk when seated he now seemed to loom above both the desk and Sally like an outsize in manpower. "I'm not in the least indifferent to anything that happens to Francie," he said with startling vehemence. "It's just that it would be . . . unfair. She'd think I was giving way, agreeing with her. Heaven knows I want to"—his flat hand struck the desk and Sally jumped—"but it wouldn't be fair to her. I know she doesn't realise the things she'd miss that she now takes for granted. All the little treats which are so much part of everyday so far as she's concerned. I'm not a poor man." He gave a brief, self-deprecating laugh. "I earn a jolly good salary here, and I'm proud of it. In any other circumstances—with any other girl—I'd feel I had something to offer, but where Francie is concerned I've so little. Her family—in this case her grandfather—is behind even this good salary of mine, and I know very well what would happen. Whatever we needed would be supplied. Not as a bribe, not for any particular reason, but because none of them could bear to see Francie waiting for or going without the things she wanted and had to save up for. I don't want that," he said, not shouting, but saying each word so that

Sally could not mistake his meaning, could not help but hear the pride in his voice.

"I want to provide for my wife and family *myself*," he said with deadly sincerity. "It's a . . . sort of 'thing' so far as I'm concerned. And I should hate to see Francie nobly doing without whatever it was she wanted to salve my pride. No," his tone dropped, became suddenly dead and lifeless. "It's better this way. I've not come to this conclusion rashly and without undue thought," he went on. "I've examined it from all angles. It's not fair to Francie, and if she won't see it for herself, then someone else has to see it for her, however much it may hurt."

Sally said nothing for a moment, and Martin began again, seeming to be speaking almost to himself.

"Some day, somewhere, she'll meet someone else who's on equal terms of living up to her standards. I only hope I've managed a best-seller before then, or an outstanding film, but"—he gave the brief laugh again, disconcerting Sally, there was so much hurt behind it—"one can't gamble on a thing like that happening."

"Have you ever thought," Sally ventured, "that maybe Francie doesn't want anything else except what only you can give her? Yourself and," she added, greatly daring, "your . . . love?"

Martin looked down on the small, determined figure and there was a faint gleam of appreciation in his eyes as he answered her.

"I think you'd better go, Miss Nesbitt," he said politely. "You put the case very well . . . too well. I'm almost inclined to weaken. It's merely the knowledge that it would be wrong to Francie to do so which holds me back." Sally rose and looked up at him, liking what she saw and wishing desperately she could help. "Tell her I'm glad she let me know," he concluded, "and that I'm sorry she's hurt. I hope with all my heart she will soon be well . . ." He turned away, just before, Sally would have staked her life, he added 'and give her my love', but he did not say the words, merely wished her good afternoon and nothing more.

CHAPTER SIX

MIKE was waiting for Sally as she emerged from Martin's room, leaning on the corridor wall and whistling faintly through his teeth. One look at her troubled face told him what he wanted to know. Thoughtfully he tucked her hand in his arm and began to propel her gently along the corridor towards the stairs.

"I take it things didn't go as you hoped?" he said, as he helped her into the car and took his place beside her.

"No." Sally spoke thoughtfully. "I'd like to help them," she surprised him by saying. "I'd like to see them happy ... Francie and her Martin."

"And what about me?" Mike parried quickly. "Wouldn't you like to see me happy? You could make me the happiest man on earth, Sally Nesbitt, and it wouldn't take much effort or time."

"Only the rest of our lives to see you wishing you hadn't been so impulsive," Sally countered swiftly. "Leave well alone, Mike. We're all right as we are."

"This love business is a funny thing." Mike made no move to drive away from the kerb. "There's Francie, you say she's eating her heart out for Martin, and with her money and looks she could go round the world and come back with a playboy or a title or both. There's Martin, obviously—since you say so—feeling just the same way about Francie as she does about him, and letting her grandfather and her father's fortune stand in the way of happiness. And here am I"—he flung his arm dramatically so that Sally began to cast anxious glances at the passers-by, wondering what they were thinking—"ready to do anything you ask of me, and all you can say is 'let's be good friends'. I like being friends with you, Sally. You're the best friend I've ever had, male or female, but it's ... well, it's gradually becoming not enough. Tell me"—he turned suddenly in his seat and faced her—"is there—anyone else? Have you met that other 'someone' you've always been convinced you'd meet up with one day?"

Just for a moment the tell-tale colour rushed into Sally's cheeks, then faded, leaving her strangely white. She could not have explained why, but at Mike's words she had a sudden but vivid mental picture of Curtis Palmer as he had looked that morning when he had called in at Francie's room for a moment. She blinked rapidly and the image vanished, but Mike had seen the hot tide of colour and had drawn his conclusions.

"There *is* someone else," he said almost accusingly, "whether you admit it or not, Sally. Do you"—despite himself and his air of uncaring carelessness his voice shook a little as he forced out the words—"want to stop . . . seeing me?" he asked slowly.

"Of course not." Sally hoped she wasn't sounding too emphatic. "If there is—anyone else, as you put it," she spoke with slow deliberation, "it isn't of any importance. It's just a case of wishful thinking that can never come true. As for wanting to stop seeing you, that's the last thing I'll ever want, Mike," she said sincerely, "even if I ever found—someone else. I value our friendship, providing it doesn't hurt *you*," she went on seriously. "If that's what's happening, maybe we'd better stop seeing each other."

"I can bear it." Mike's usual grin was back in its accustomed place and he made a great business of starting the car. "I think I can bear most things, if we're going together, Sally. The bad time will come when you find that 'someone else' and he finds you, both at the same time." He grinned down at her suddenly. "We're getting too serious," he announced. "This isn't us. Let's go and eat and then go to the Gaumont. There's a new thriller there; we'll just have time to see it round before I have to take you back to purdah."

"I can catch the bus," Sally said quickly. "It's a long way out for you . . . and I thought you said you had another job to cover?"

"Young Lenton's offered to go, so I let him." Mike pulled up in the car park behind the Copper Bowl. "I'll double for him some time when he wants to take his best girl out."

Sally smiled and said nothing, following Mike's bulky figure into the little restaurant, but all the same she felt strangely sad, troubled and ill at ease, something which rarely happened when she was with Mike.

'Must be the double effect of Martin Howbury refusing to come and see Francie, even though it's perfectly obvious he's dying to see her, and then Mike turning serious again. It's not like him. He usually waits a month or so before he has a second try.'

She stole a glance at him over the table. With all her heart she wished suddenly that he didn't remind her so much of her brother and that she could think of him as he wanted her to think of him, not as another brother like Paul, but as someone special, someone outside her ordinary family life.

'In short, Sally Nesbitt,' she told herself firmly, 'you wish you *could* fall in love with Mike, instead of realising, as you should, that's something you'll never be able to do, dear as he is to you. And as for thinking of Curtis Palmer . . . he doesn't come to see me, he calls in to see Francie . . . and if he calls far more frequently than is necessary, don't let yourself believe it's for any other reason than to see the patient . . .'

"And there was the man, on top of the ladder . . ." Sally gathered her wandering thoughts together, realising with a start that Mike had given their order and was in the throes of telling her some story about his work and that she had not even paid him the compliment of listening. With an effort she focused her attention on what Mike was saying, and in a short time all her worrying thoughts were forgotten as Mike, with his usual easy talk, told her story after story of the happenings of the week which had made up the news of the district.

They walked the short distance from the Copper Bowl to the cinema, and watched the film in comparative silence. Mike bought some of Sally's favourite mint cream chocolates, and once, when his fingers casually curled round hers, she almost drew them away, but he seemed content enough to let her hand simply lie in his, and in the end she left it there.

It was dark when they emerged, and a glance at her watch told Sally there would be no time for a coffee after the show unless she wanted to invite trouble. Despite her protests that the bus stopped outside the nurses' home, Mike was insistent that he should take her back, and at last, after not a great deal of protest, Sally agreed.

The drive back was pleasant. Mike knew of and respected her wishes for being driven more slowly at night, and shortly before ten-thirty he pulled up at the gates of the nurses' home.

"See you on Sunday?" he asked, as she got out of the car. "You said you had the whole day free, so I wondered if you'd like to go home. Give the folks a surprise, as it were. Do you think they'd mind if I showed up again?"

"They'd be delighted to have you," Sally told him. "The twins think you're tops, Mum and Dad like you and Paul and you get on fine." In case he got any wrong ideas she added hastily: "Sue and her boy friend will be home. We could make up a four . . . the tennis courts are open now."

"Right." Mike let in the clutch, and Sally was thankful he had evidently decided it was not worth while to make another attempt towards sentiment that evening. "See you Sunday," he said cheerily. "Don't let your patients get you down!" Then he turned the car and with a further wave of his hand was off back down the road to Barcaster.

Sally walked slowly down the drive-way to the doors of the home, wishing again she could give Mike the answer he wanted. He was such a grand chap, in every way, and she thought the world of him, but not in the way he hoped for.

"You're too fussy," Betty had said once. "You want the sort of love story you read about in books, and I'm sure that doesn't happen more than once in a blue moon in real life. I'd settle for someone with whom I got on as well as you get on with Mike, who thought the world of me. It beats you thinking the world of him . . . they say there's always one who loves and one who is loved," she had quoted seriously. "I intend being the one who's loved . . . less wearing!"

Sally had almost reached the doors of the home as these thoughts crossed her mind, and at first she thought that the slight figure in the dark checked coat, huddled into the thick shrubbery, was a figment of her imagination, culled from her thoughts of her friend, but as she neared the girl she caught the sound of a stifled sob and in an instant she was off the path, her arms reaching out to the other, who still half turned away.

"Betty?" she called softly, anxiously. "What's wrong? It's Sally, love. Tell me what's the matter."

It was some time before the agitated Betty could control her tears sufficiently to talk coherently. When at last she was able to distinguish the words Betty discovered her friend had been late for her appointment with Pete.

"I'm always a few minutes late, on principle," Betty sniffed disconsolately. "He has so many girls running after him all the time I think I shouldn't let him think he . . . matters as much as all that, being there first and waiting for him, like a parcel," she ended on a faint note of indignation.

"But it does matter, doesn't it?" Sally queried softly, her arm about her friend. "You like Pete more than you like anyone else, don't you?"

"I like him better than anyone else in the world," Betty announced with an emphasis which surprised Sally, accustomed to her friend's casual acceptance of the boys who made up her numerous acquaintances. "And I didn't know, not until today, I think"—she raised a mournful face to Sally's and a tear still trembled on her lashes—"I think I *love* him . . . and I've just found out when I've lost him."

"It can't be as bad as all that," Sally protested, more shaken than she would have cared to admit by the sight of her usually happy-go-lucky friend looking so miserable and woebegone. "You and Pete have been going around together for ages. He's been taking you out far longer than he's taken anyone else. What's it all about?"

"I kept him waiting longer than usual today," Betty began. "I really didn't mean to be as late as that, but Sister Bellairs saw me in the hall and stopped to ask me something. She talks—you know how she talks—and by the time I got away it was just in time to see Pete giving a lift to that new redheaded nurse who's in the women's medical . . . Cartwright, or something. I bet he took *her* to the gliding, just because I said last week it was time we found something else for a change."

"You certainly seem to have felt sure of him . . . until now," Sally said gently. "Let's go in and have a coffee and talk over what you can do to put matters right."

She tucked her arm reassuringly in Betty's, giving the other girl an affectionate squeeze.

"The first thing," she said slowly, "is to ring Pete up as soon as you've had your coffee—before you go up to bed —and to apologise for being so late. Explain that Sister kept you, but don't say anything about seeing him drive off with Nurse Cartwright. I wouldn't let him know you knew," she said solemnly. "Let him think you imagine he got tired of waiting and went off on his own."

"It must be nice, having someone so dependable as Mike always there," Betty sighed as they went indoors. "Mike would wait for ever, if he thought you were coming."

"He'd know there was really something wrong if I arrived late," Sally informed her crisply. "I'm usually dead on time. It's only fair. He doesn't want to be kept hanging around any more than I do. Mike wouldn't wait 'for ever', not for any girl," she assured Betty. "No man worth his salt would, in my opinion. Love doesn't really enter into it. It's politeness and common courtesy which count, and I think we owe that to whoever we go out with, boy-friend or girl-friend. It's only fair."

"You're a funny girl, Sally," Betty said unexpectedly. "You don't bother with anyone else, only Mike, and you say you aren't in love with him, but you wouldn't be late . . ."

"They're my principles." Sally grinned and went off for

the coffee. "I just like fair play and good manners all round. It's the way my mother brought us up!"

She was soon back with the strong, hot coffee they both loved, lit two cigarettes and chatted with Betty until she was sure the other girl had regained her composure. Then she picked up the cups to return to the kitchen on her way out, and suggested: "You go and telephone Pete. Tell him how sorry you are and that it was something which you couldn't help this time. Don't mention the red-head, don't reproach him. Just be your usual sunny self—when you've apologised, of course—and see what happens. I'm going to pop down to see Miss Bodman for a moment. I said I would, then I'm for bed."

"Wish me luck, Sally." Betty was serious, not joking as usual. "This really matters to me."

"Then say your words as though you meant them," Sally advised. "It's my opinion Pete thinks the world of you, but he wouldn't think you were very keen on him if you've been late every week, 'on principle', and if you're not really keen on the things he finds interesting."

"I'll remember." Betty began to smile. "Sorry I was such an ass, but it's been my first free day without Pete for ages, and I was walking down the drive when it suddenly occurred to me why I felt so lost and lorn, even though I'd spent the afternoon at the bowling alley with Mendip and Evans and three boys from Block B."

"Make up your mind it won't happen again," Sally advised. "See you later," then she went on down the connecting drive-way to the hospital.

Strictly speaking, she had no reasonable excuse for being at Francie's private ward at this time and on her off-duty afternoon, but she had promised Francie she would let her know if she had anything to report, and she knew the other girl would be eagerly awaiting her news, perhaps, even, would not sleep unless she knew what had happened.

Francie *was* lying awake. She turned her head as Sally entered and the nurse could see the marks of strain on the lovely face.

"Did you see him?" she began. "What did he say?"

"He said how sorry he was," Sally told her carefully. "He was relieved you weren't badly hurt and he hopes you'll soon recover."

"Did he . . . did he send his love?" Francie said the words slowly and deliberately, challenging Sally to answer truthfully.

"No," Sally said slowly, almost painfully. "He didn't. But he did say he felt a bit guilty about what had happened. He felt he should have seen you home."

"He mustn't blame himself, not at all," Francie said quickly. "Nothing of this was his fault. I went where I knew no one would think of looking for me, that was all."

"He said he wasn't . . . indifferent to *anything* that happened to you," Sally went on, not sure how much of this Martin would want her to repeat. "He said it wouldn't be fair to you to come and see you—that it would only make you think he was coming over to your line of thought and that he could never do that because it would not be fair to you to expect you to live on what he makes. He didn't say it as though it were any reflection on you," she added quickly. "I suppose it's simply that he knows better than you do how hard it would be for you to adjust your standard of living to his. Though he did say his salary was a good one, it still, apparently, won't compare."

"I don't care about that," Francie said unexpectedly. "I'm tired of expensive holidays, of clothes no one sees but myself. I'm tired of all the 'treats' they plan for me, as though I'm a child. Life is for living, and Martin and people like him—people like yourself—are the ones who live, not those wrapped up in a cocoon and protected from everything and everybody.'

"Hush, now, hush," Sally insisted soothingly. "You'll send your temperature up if you carry on like that. I'll go and see him again," she announced rashly, "when you're up to having a few more visitors. Right now your parents are enough."

"They would let Martin in if he did come, wouldn't they, Nurse? I mean . . . it would help me such a lot."

"I'm sure they would." Sally made a mental note to have a word with Sister Trask on this score. "And now," she went on firmly, tucking the clothes which Francie had disturbed about the slim, prone figure, "you must try and go to sleep. At least you know he's not . . . 'indifferent' to you in any way." She smiled, but there was no answering smile on the face of the girl in the bed. "I'll see he's kept informed of your progress," she said, as she went back to the door. "I don't say I shall be any more successful than I've been today, but if we can get him to pop over, promise there won't be any scene?"

"There won't be any scene," Francie said so seriously that Sally believed her implicitly. "I only want to *see* him, you see," she added wistfully. "I thought if he saw me like this"—she gestured down the bed—"he might be sorry . . . wish he'd agreed . . . but I wouldn't make any sort of a scene," she said again. "It would only upset Martin, achieve no useful purpose and probably get you into trouble as well. Besides," she added suddenly, "it's against my principles."

The angry words which rose, almost unbidden, to Sally's tongue were bitten back by sheer effort of will power. She began to think she had heard enough of other people's principles for one day. Instead she said brightly:

"We'll see what we can do," and went out, closing the door softly behind her, but as she walked slowly back to the nurses' home her heart was filled with pity for the lovely girl who, on the face of things, appeared to have in abundance everything which life could offer and yet who was eating her heart out for the love of one man who was also—Sally's natural good humour returned and she giggled—hurting them both by what she was certain he would also refer to as 'my principles'.

'It's a funny old world,' she told herself as she went quietly up to her room. 'Or maybe it's just the folks in it.' She stifled a yawn. 'And now for Betty . . . and what she's made of her little affair. Let's hope there's a happy ending for *somebody*!'

CHAPTER SEVEN

SALLY woke bright and early the following morning feeling considerably less depressed. Betty had been waiting for her the previous evening, full of thanks and expressions of gratitude, for Pete, it seemed, was even less happy about the afternoon—which had not, after all, been spent in the company of the new nurse but alone—than Betty had been. They had arranged to meet on the following Saturday, when Betty's next free time coincided with Pete's, and by the smile on her face and the happiness in her eyes Sally felt she need have no further doubts about the future of her friend and her current love affair.

'I wish things could work out just as well for Francie and her Martin,' she thought, as she opened the door of Francie's room, then stopped short. "I beg your pardon, sir," she was beginning, but as he rose from the chair beside the bed, Curtis Palmer gave her a welcoming, friendly smile.

"I looked in to see Miss Bodman, Nurse," he explained. "As I've just been telling her, I think she'll soon be ready for the physio people and learning to walk again. There's movement in the toes of both feet," he went on, explaining in medical detail which was quite incomprehensible to Francie but which appeared to please Sally very much. "It will be quite a long job," he concluded, "but a very satisfactory one when completed, I feel sure." He paused for a moment on his way to the door and turned back to look once again directly into Sally's eyes.

"I've been most pleased to learn you suffered no ill-effects from your impromptu dive, Nurse," he said primly. "It must have taken a great deal of courage, and there could have been some very nasty after-effects for you personally, you know."

"I didn't even think about it," Sally confessed, feeling the warm colour rise in her cheeks under his direct gaze. "I'm afraid it didn't occur to me . . . and anyway," she ended lamely, "I've been lucky."

"Lucky *and* plucky," Curtis smiled, evidently pleased with his own small attempt at humour. "Anyhow, I would like you to know how pleased I am things turned out so well . . . for you both."

"Thank you," Sally said demurely, holding open the door as became her position, but he stopped again.

"By the way," he said, as though this were an afterthought, "if you—and, I suppose, your friend, of course—are really interested in flowers and what-have-you, my mother has a wonderful display of some special orchids just coming into flower in the hothouse. If you would care to see them, I'm sure you would be most welcome. She asked me to tell you," he ended, and had he been anyone else Sally would have thought he had spoken in some confusion.

"Thank you," she said again. "I'll tell Mike. It should be an item of interest for his column."

"Oh, yes, I'd forgotten. You said he was a reporter, I believe. Hmm." For a moment the blue-grey eyes searched Sally's sherry-brown ones with an expression she could not quite fathom, but it was quickly gone. "Anyhow, I'll tell Mother I mentioned it," he said abruptly, and the next moment he was gone, striding down the corridor, broad shoulders squared, as if, thought Sally ridiculously, he were marching into battle.

From the bed, Francie gave a little giggle. Glancing round at her patient, Sally raised an eyebrow.

"He's sweet and he's shy," Francie said slowly. "Fancy a man who can, and does, do all the wonderful things he can do, being shy when he comes to see a patient. I guess he doesn't think of patients as people," she said earnestly, "or nurses as women. When he realises they are—in either case—he just bolts."

"My own view exactly," Sally agreed, "but he's rather nice," she went on, methodically taking Francie's temperature and recording it, but as she worked her heart sank. For one moment she had felt that perhaps Curtis Palmer had called in to see *her*, knowing she was being held responsible for Francie, then she dismissed the idea. Had he not just mentioned Mike, not by name, but by implication that 'her friend' would be just as interested in the orchids as Sally would be? Had his mother made the suggestion of a visit, or had he? And if so, why?

'Don't be an ass,' she told herself sternly, and brought her mind sharply back to the work in hand. 'He's been in to see Francie and for no other reason. After all, Sister Trask was saying how much Curtis wanted some new and special equipment. With Francie's grandfather as Chairman and with all that money behind him, it's only policy that she should receive just a little special attention, personal visits and contacts more than necessary and all that sort of thing.'

"Sally!" She looked round, startled, for although Francie had asked the previous day if she might use her nurse's Christian name this was the first time she had done so. "You are my friend, aren't you?" she asked.

"Of course," Sally spoke with assurance. Apart from the fact that Francie was obviously in need of a friend, a confidante, and felt in an extreme sense that she was both grateful to and dependent upon Sally, she really had grown to like the other girl more than she would have thought it possible to like anyone else other than Betty. "You know I am," she went on now. "Why do you ask?"

"Flowers for Miss Bodman. Came by special messenger." There was a light tap on the door, and before Sally had time to call 'Come in' a young cadet had entered carrying the most beautiful bouquet of flowers Sally had ever seen. In seconds their perfume had filled the small room. Francie stretched out her arms for them, and obediently Sally placed the bouquet within her grasp.

"There's a card, Sally," Francie said quickly. "Get it off for me, will you, please."

Sally dismissed the cadet, saying she would put the flowers in water herself, then briskly detached the white envelope from the wire which bound it to the bouquet.

"You hold the flowers a minute, will you, Sally, please?"

Willingly Sally took the beautiful bouquet into her arms, burying her face in the perfumed sweetness for a moment. Suddenly Francie spoke again.

"They're from Martin," she said, in a strained little voice. "Listen. It says, '*The flowers speak my message. Get well soon. Martin.*' That's all. Do you know anything about the language of flowers, Sally? There is one, I know . . ." Francie wrinkled her brow, concentrating. "All I can remember is red roses for love," she announced in self-disgust. "There aren't any red roses here . . ."

"There's white lilac, rosemary and pink camellias," Sally examined the skilfully made-up bouquet carefully. "And the foliage, of course. I don't know about that, but I'm pretty sure Mavis Trane will have a book on the language of flowers if there's one to be had. I can find out for you."

"Who's Mavis Trane, and when can you find out?" Francie demanded. "There must be a meaning, or Martin wouldn't have written those words on the card."

"Mavis does the women's page in the *Chronicle* every week. I can ring her at the office in my lunch hour and ask, if you like."

"Please," Francie begged. "I know he's tried to say something here, but what?"

"We'll find out when I have my luncheon break," Sally promised. "Now, what about a spot of massage? Let me help you turn over."

"I was asking about you meaning it when you said you'd be my friend," Francie reminded her as Sally began her work. "Remember?"

"I remember," Sally assured her. "And I said 'yes'," she placed definite emphasis on the word, feeling that somehow her patient was suddenly in need of assurance. Why?"

"You won't let them take me away from here, will you, Sally?" was the next astounding question. "Mummy and Daddy, I mean."

"But surely they wouldn't want to do *that* !" Sally was bewildered. "You're getting on so well. I know there's a lot to be done yet before you're as fit as you were, but that's only a matter of time and rest."

"I know that," Francie said impatiently, "and they know it too. They've been talking to someone they know

ance the problem would, miraculously, be solved. "Can you send him a telegram or something? I bet they haven't let him know about this, or he'd have been over, but," for a moment she sounded almost mischievous, "although they love him dearly and let him take the lead in almost everything, I sometimes think they're a wee bit jealous because he and I get on so well all the time. I remind him of Grandma, you see, the only one in the entire family who resembles her in the least, and I'm exactly like her, or so they say. And he adored her. Because of that he'll do almost anything for me . . ."

"I don't know," Sally began doubtfully, but at that moment Francie's mid-morning drink was brought in by one of the local voluntary workers who helped out at the General from time to time.

"Sally," Francie began, "Mrs. Parsons is an old friend. She often does special sewing for Mummy. Do you mind if we chat a few minutes and you run up to wherever it is you go and try to telephone Mavis Trane? Mrs. Parsons will get some vases. There are plenty in that cupboard." She pointed. "Nurse Pearson told me so the other day."

Knowing how anxious the other girl was to read the message in the bouquet of flowers, Sally allowed herself to be persuaded. Francie would be quite all right with Mrs. Parsons there, and it would do her good to have someone else to talk to for a change.

It did not take long to get through to Mike at the office. Fortunately she caught him in.

"Only popped in for a moment to hand in this for the early edition," he told her breezily, "but it's always grand to hear from you, Sally. What can I do for you?"

It was not long before he had connected her with the phone on Mavis Trane's desk, and in a second or two Sally heard the brisk, soft voice of the smart girl reporter she had already met several times.

"Good heavens!" Mavis exclaimed when Sally had explained her mission. "I thought that sort of thing was out of date. Be quite a thing if this starts a revival. Hang on a minute while I look this up. I have a little chart thing somewhere in my desk."

The explanation was simple, when Mavis finally found the 'little chart thing', but Sally did not think it was one calculated to bring much joy to Francie's heart.

"White lilac," Mavis told her, "stands for innocence, purity and all that. In this case I should say the sender puts the girl on rather a pedestal. Am I right?"

"I don't know them well enough," Sally evaded. "It's a patient of mine who received the flowers this morning and wanted to know if the flowers chosen had any special significance."

"All flowers have 'special significance', if people only think about it," Mavis said crisply. "I'm glad whoever your patient is had the sense to see they must have been especially chosen. Now, what did you say next? Rosemary? That's for remembrance. Doesn't sound too good. Sounds as if whoever he is is saying a fond farewell. And then camellias ... pink ones ... let me see."

She had the last flower in a matter of moments, but she sounded as disappointed as Sally felt as she listened.

"Loveliness," Mavis said slowly. "Sounds to me as though he worships her and doesn't think himself good enough, so he's saying a perfumed farewell. Someone ought to tell him he's making a mistake; a man who takes all that thought and trouble to bid a girl goodbye isn't lightly come by these days."

Privately Sally agreed with her, but she could hardly inform Mavis that she was speaking of her editor, so with another word of thanks she hung up, asking Mavis to tell Mike she hadn't time to prolong the call, then she headed back to Francie's small private ward wondering how she could give the girl the message in a way which would hurt the least.

Mrs. Parsons was ready to leave as Sally entered, and with a final cheery word to the girl in the bed she went on her way. No sooner had the door closed behind her than Francie asked:

"Well, did you find anything about it, and what do they mean? Do they really translate into any sort of message?"

"I'm afraid they do," Sally said slowly, consulting the

notes she had made as Mavis talked. "White lilac means he thinks you're beautiful . . . no, sorry, that means innocence. He worships you like someone on a pedestal. Rosemary is for remembrance . . . even I knew that, shades of *Hamlet*, I believe, something of Shakespeare's I learned at school, anyhow. The camellias mean loveliness, so the conclusion is that he adores your beauty and innocence, but feels he just isn't good enough for you . . . which you know already . . . so he's saying he'll remember you always. Just that and no more."

Francie was silent so long that Sally wondered if she had heard and understood what had been said, but at last she spoke, her voice low and controlled, startling Sally by the evident resolve in its depths.

"I shall find a way to make him change his mind," Francie said slowly. "There has to be a way . . . and this is something Grandpa can't help with. If he interfered Martin would get a job somewhere else, and all that would mean would be that he'd be working where he wasn't happy—perhaps not being as well paid, not with the paper and the people he loves—and Grandpa would lose a good editor. No"—her small fist smote the bedcovers hard—"this is something I've got to do for myself. And you'll have to help me, Sally," she said firmly. "I don't know how, yet, but there'll be a way if we look hard enough for one. You will help, won't you?" she ended, pathetically eager.

"I will, if I can," Sally said cautiously, "but . . ." Before she could get any further with what she intended to say the door opened and Stella Bodman stood there, her wide mouth breaking into a smile as she crossed to where Francie lay.

"I've telephoned the Matron at The Mount," she began, "and she has a bed ready for you. Mr. Johnson will look after you there. I hear he's very good."

CHAPTER EIGHT

SALLY hesitated by the door. She ought to leave mother and daughter alone for a little while, but something in the appealing glance Francie cast in her direction halted her steps.

"I'm not going, Mother," Francie said slowly and distinctly, two bright spots of colour appearing on her cheekbones as she made this defiant statement. "I don't want to leave here until they've finished with me, until they've done all they can for me, and by that time I'll be better."

"I hope so." Stella Bodman gave a disparaging glance upwards at the exercising pulley rigged up above Francie's bed. "It seems to be taking a dreadfully long time," she was beginning doubtfully, when Francie appealed directly to Sally.

"Everyone here is pleased with me, aren't they, Nurse?" she demanded. "Mr. Palmer, Miss Trevelyan— she's the physio lady, Mummy—*everyone*," she said again emphatically. "I start to learn to walk again next week. Miss Trevelyan says it will be as well to go on with the massage for a time, to tone up the muscles or something. It seems they were badly weakened, but they are getting stronger. It isn't really that, though," she amended honestly. "I just don't want to leave Sally. I've never made a friend before, and now I have and I like it. Sally wouldn't work at The Mount if she could, not just now. She likes it here, and so do I. But most of all I want to stay where Sally is. And, if she'll come, I want her to come to Queen's Close on a visit as soon as I'm better."

"And who," Stella asked in slightly amused tones, "is Sally?"

"This is Sally." Francie stretched out her hand and, pink-cheeked at this unexpected introduction, Sally allowed herself to be drawn nearer to the bedside. "It was Sally who pulled me from the river, you know, Mummy. And she's been the one who's done the most looking after me. She's wonderful!"

"Shush!" Sally remonstrated with Francie quietly, wondering what sort of effect all this was going to have on Mrs. Bodman. "I've only done my duty," she addressed the older woman, "but I must admit I've grown very fond of your daughter too," she added briefly.

"I remember you." Stella wrinkled her brows. "Forgive me, my dear," she continued charmingly, "you must think me very rude, but the events of that night are somewhat confused in my mind. I ought to have recognised you . . ."

"I understand." Sally smiled, and at that moment the door opened, making Stella turn in surprise.

"What now?" she demanded. "I always seem to come in at the wrong time," she said fretfully. "That was why I wanted you at The Mount, Sally. When Grandma was there we could go in and out at any hour of the day. Nobody said anything, although they didn't particularly like you there at meal-times, but if it so happened it *was* a meal-time when one called one was always invited to take a cup of tea."

"I don't know whether we can manage anything, Mrs. Bodman," Sally began doubtfully, "but this is Francie's luncheon, and Cadet Mason usually looks after her while I go for mine. I could try in the kitchen and see if I can get you a cup of coffee when they make it," she offered doubtfully. "I take it someone knows you're here?"

"A rather stern-looking Sister reminded me that yesterday Matron had told me we should use the ordinary visiting hours," Stella said happily, "but I don't really see I'm doing any harm. You run along and have your own meal, Nurse. I'll look after my daughter . . ." and although Sally would have liked to have explained that Francie's back was still not strong enough to allow her to sit up and feed herself, Stella looked so determined that, with a slight shrug of her shoulders, she went out and left them to it.

Betty was already at their table when Sally reached the dining-room, and as soon as the meal was served the two friends began to chatter as though they hadn't met for years.

"Pete was on our ward this morning," Betty began. "He

did the rounds with Mr. Stampton. He winked at me twice when he shouldn't have done. I almost gave us both away."

"Mr. Stampton can't bear frivolous behaviour," Sally observed mechanically. "He says it reflects badly on the standards of the hospital. Really, Betty, you ought to think of Pete a little bit, even if he won't be serious himself. It's up to you to make him see there is a time for fun and . . ."

"A time for loving . . . I know, it's all in the Good Book," Betty grinned mischievously. "But what's life without laughter?" she countered quickly. "It does you good. What about you, love? Anything new on your front this morning?"

"Odds and ends," Sally said noncommittally. "Martin sent Francie a beautiful bouquet of flowers, and a 'get well soon' card, and added the cryptic comment that the flowers carried his message."

"What were they?" Betty asked, her eyes dancing. "Red roses for love, I suppose?"

"Nothing of the kind." Sally frowned, remembering how much value Francie had placed on this perfumed message and how disappointed she must have been when it was translated for her. "They were a mixture of camellias—pink ones—white lilac and rosemary. When it was put together what it meant was that he has a boundless love for her beauty and innocence, that he puts her on a pedestal and is content to worship from afar, doesn't consider himself good enough and so is saying he won't forget her but this is goodbye."

"And what's she doing about it?" Betty asked. "From what you told me she thinks the world of him. She must do, if she had to go where she did to think out what was best to do next."

"She thinks the world of him," Sally said slowly, "but what can she do? You can't force a man to marry you, not like that. You can't force him to see you, if he thinks it better for both of you if he doesn't."

"She could try going into a decline," Betty said, but not very seriously. "I know that's out of date, but when her parents saw what was happening I think they're the type to relent."

"I don't think there is or would be any parental opposition," Sally confessed, finishing off the last of her pudding. "On the contrary, I gather the whole family like him, think he's tops at his job, and the grandfather thinks he's the best editor he's ever had. I think they'd welcome him with arms so wide open they'd frighten him farther away, if you know what I mean. They'd think they could *buy* him for her, and that's just what he's afraid of."

"Sticky business," Betty commented. "We'll have to give it some thought. Your little Francie sounds too nice a kid to leave around carrying a torch for someone who's evidently very worthy of it but just doesn't appear to want it. And what's Curtis Palmer doing, spending so much time down in that small private ward?" she asked impishly. "I know your little patient is under his care, but she should be past the stage of long, complicated visits by this time. What's the attraction?" Betty teased. "Patient or nurse?"

"You know perfectly well he's only doing his job," Sally retorted with more than a touch of asperity. "Curtis Palmer is a good surgeon. Francesca Bodman had a very nasty fall. She was concussed for days . . . anything might have developed. Anything still might, with a spine as badly contused as hers was. Miss Trevelyan feels they've done wonders, but there's still a long way to go. This weekend they're getting her out to the pre-walking stage. It takes time, you know, Betty . . . or are you fooling?" she ended suspiciously as she caught sight of the twinkle in the depths of her friend's green eyes.

"Fooling, just a little," Betty confessed. "But I know what you think of Curtis. You're as bad as the rest of them now, it shows in your eyes. And a little bird told me he'd invited you to his home to see his mother's orchids."

"After a paragraph in the gossip column of the *Chronicle*," Sally announced shortly, not at all sure she was speaking the truth. If she were honest she would have to admit that she did not believe Curtis would extend the invitation for any such reason. "He asked me to take my 'newspaper friend' along as well," she explained.

"In that case he must be after impressing the Bodmans to get his new equipment." Betty was not to be dashed. "There's something in it. He's always hanging round your part of the hospital these days."

"You've an overworked imagination," Sally told her crisply. "You ought to be writing books. I've got to get back," she announced as the scraping of chairs heralded the end of lunchtime. "I've left Mrs. Bodman there with Francie. She—Mrs. B., I mean—seems to think we ought to run a special service for visitors, cups of tea and what have you."

"I've no doubt she'll get it." Betty rose too. "The Mrs. Bodmans of this world always appear to get what they want whoever must be sacrificed to that end. But don't forget," she warned her friend as they parted to go their separate ways, "you mustn't let her order *you* about. Think of the dignity of the profession!" And with a last merry wave of her hand she was off, humming to herself, being out of earshot of authority.

Sally walked briskly but demurely back to the small ward where Francie Bodman lay, smiling to herself as she thought how quickly Betty had recovered from what she had firmly believed was a broken heart the day Pete had taken the new redheaded nurse out in her stead.

'And he hadn't, after all,' Sally remembered, still smiling. 'Anyhow, it's apparently taught them both a lesson, Betty *and* Pete.'

"You look very pleased with yourself, Staff." Sally gave a start of surprise as Curtis drew abreast of her and fell into step by her side. "You really are devoted to your work, aren't you?" he went on, rather startling Sally. "You don't waste a minute . . . in gossip with your friends or anything else . . . always on the job."

'He's been watching me!' The thought crossed Sally's mind exultantly until, coming back to earth with a mental bump, she reminded herself that what Betty had said was true and that Curtis had spent so much time in

Francie's ward that he was bound to have noticed Sally at least some of the time.

"I only do what's expected of me," she said primly. "Miss Bodman is going along nicely now, but it *was* a bit tricky at first. Obviously she had something on her mind."

"Most people have," Curtis said briefly, and to Sally's genuine amazement he at once turned the topic of conversation. Evidently he did not, after all, wish to talk of Francie.

"Tell me, Staff"—he halted in the corridor just a little way from the door of Francie's room—"what else do you like to do in your free time besides attend flower shows and gymkhanas?" Sally must have looked as startled as she felt, for she had not seen him at the gymkhana, but he smiled and said, in explanation: "My young niece was riding in the pony-jumping. Mother went to see her, and she told me you were there."

"I see." Sally pondered a moment. "I . . . do almost anything," she said simply. "It all depends . . ."

"On what assignment—isn't that what they call it?—your young newspaper friend has in hand, I suppose?" Curtis said rather too quickly, and turned away.

Sally wanted to take him by the arm of his coat and tell him she only went on these excursions with Mike because he enjoyed having her with him and that she usually enjoyed the different functions they attended together, even if Mike were in his official capacity, but that there was nothing serious about it. That this was just friendship, at least so far as she was concerned, but Sister Ashley was just coming down the corridor and she would have frowned upon such a performance by one of the staff nurses. And anyway, Sally thought miserably, might not Curtis have frowned upon it too?

"I'll just have a word with Miss Bodman," he was saying now as he opened the door to Francie's room. "The periods of confused thinking, of a mixed-up emotional state are less and less frequent, I understand," he went on crisply, "and I think, according to Miss Trevelyan, she ought to be able to try walking with the crutches at the beginning of next week."

Sally was following him into the room feeling very much in a 'mixed-up emotional state' herself. Was she wrong, or had he been about to make some suggestion that they spent some of their free time together? Was he, her heart beat faster and the blood seemed to pound along her veins, about to give some invitation for her next free day when she had, quite without thinking, led him to believe that her free time was irrevocably bound up with Mike Amberton?

'Idiot!' she chided herself mentally. 'You'll never get him round to where he'll say anything like that again . . . or at least not for ages.'

She was desperately searching for the words which would give him the opportunity of issuing such an invitation if he so wished, words which would tell him she was by no means the property of Mike, whatever circumstances may hint, when she was aware there was a conversation already going on in the small room. Stella Bodman had risen from the chair by the bed, and Sally noted with some inward amusement that someone had evidently been brave enough to venture to the kitchen and procure the desired cup of tea, for the empty cup stood in its saucer where Stella had been sitting.

"I know it isn't official visiting time, Mr. Palmer," she was saying in her deep, authoritative voice, "but so far we have been accorded a few privileges. We shall not take advantage of them for very much longer, I do assure you. I was explaining to Francie what we have done and why, when you came in."

"And what *have* you done, Mrs. Bodman?" Curtis asked quietly, "and why have you done it . . . whatever it is?"

"Why"—Stella waved her hands in an airy gesture which would have looked charming in her daughter but rather ridiculous when performed by Stella—"I've telephoned the Matron at The Mount," she explained. "She's an old friend of ours. Grandma was there for some time, you see, and we came to know the staff rather well. I've told Francie there is a bed ready for her there, and that Mr. Johnson will be looking after her. He's very good, you know," she added, while Sally inwardly trembled.

"I know Julian Johnson is very good, Mrs. Bodman," Curtis was saying politely, "and, of course, if you wish to take your daughter from us there is nothing we can do about it, but"—he glanced at Francie, who seemed to be struggling for expression, and then back at her mother— "what does my patient feel about it?" he enquired in a more gentle tone.

"Francie is being silly and just a little thoughtless," her mother said briskly. "She says she doesn't want to go —she doesn't want to leave this hospital, nor this particular nurse. I can well understand that," she said emphatically. "After all, as we all know, Nurse Nesbitt saved her life, but what she fails to realise is that I cannot go on, day after day, not being able to see her except at the ridiculous times your rules specify, and only for a matter of half an hour or so then. As I have said, Matron and the staff here have been most kind, but . . ." Again the vague, deprecating gesture. "I have felt a little uncomfortable on my last three visits—nothing to complain about, really, I suppose," she added hastily as Curtis seemed about to speak, "but I've felt in the way, and so I tell her it will be better for all of us if she is taken to The Mount this afternoon."

"I see." Curtis did not say any more for the moment. He crossed to the bedside and leaned over the girl who lay there, watching him closely, her violet-blue eyes enormous in her white face. "And what have you to say about it, Francie?" he asked gently. "You have heard what your mother says. We cannot keep you here if you wish to go, but we shall be sorry to lose you, before you are fit to leave us."

Sally felt her heart ache for the other girl. Stella Bodman knew nothing of the confused state of mind which always attended these cases and she could have no possible idea of the really hard fight Francie had put up to bring herself as far along the road to recovery as she had done already. Now much of the work of patient, doctor and nurse alike might well be undone in a matter of moments.

When at last Francesca spoke it was with a tremendous effort, but every word was clear and made excellent sense.

"I don't want to go," she said distinctly. "I don't want to go to any other hospital. When I leave here I want to go home. And I want Sally to come with me . . . on a holiday. I don't want to leave Sally," she insisted, and she turned her head on the pillow until her gaze caught and held Sally's own. "I want Sally with me until I'm well. She helps me so much."

"Who does, my precious." They all looked round. Stella, Curtis, Sally, even Francesca's glance went from Sally to the figure by the door, and when she saw who it was her eyes lit up and a smile of happiness and relief transformed her face as she lifted her arms in welcome.

"Grandpa!" she exclaimed in a tone of sheer disbelief. "You weren't due home yet!"

The short, stocky figure of the elderly man advanced towards the bed, and he nodded briskly to his daughter-in-law and to Curtis as he did so, while the bright blue eyes under their bushy white eyebrows took in every detail of Sally's trim appearance before he stooped to gather his granddaughter into his arms.

"Who helps you, my pet?" he asked again. "And in what way?"

"In every way," Francie said in a voice scarcely above a whisper, but the old man heard every word. "That's Sally"—her eyes indicated the nurse—"and she saved my life to begin with and now she's helping me get better. She won't let me believe I can't, she's really putting life into me, and I won't be parted from her." Her voice rose again on a note of hysteria, and Sally took a step forward, all her professional instincts aroused by so much upsetting emotion, but the old gentleman did not seem disturbed. Tenderly he stroked Francie's cheek for a moment, then turned to Curtis, whom he evidently knew quite well.

"No use being in my position if there isn't something one can do to help, is it, Mr. Palmer?" he asked quietly. "Suppose you and I have a quiet word or two in the corridor. I think we shall be able to come to some arrangement suitable to everyone."

He turned back to Francie, his eyes twinkling, and gently he laid her hand back on the covers.

"Be a good girl for a few minutes, love," he counselled, "and we'll see what we can do to help. Matron has told me all about it, and I think she'll be on our side. If you could spare a minute or so, Mr. Palmer?" he invited, and the next minute the door closed behind the two men while Sally looked from mother to daughter and wondered what might happen next.

CHAPTER NINE

SALLY need not have worried. As soon as the door had closed behind Sam Bodman and Curtis, Stella sank back on the chair beside the bed, a faint smile playing about her mouth.

"It isn't any use my saying any more," she announced, but she did not seem in the least resentful. "Your grandfather will arrange something. He always does, and whatever it is it will turn out to be the best for everyone, so we can only wait and see."

Ignoring Sally, who busied herself about the room, Stella went on to talk to her daughter about a holiday she and her husband had been planning for 'when you're strong enough, darling', but the girl did not appear to be interested. She kept her gaze on the door which had closed behind the two men, but every now and again her anxious glance sought Sally's, as though seeking reassurance.

They were gone a long time, but when they returned Curtis only looked in for a moment, glancing at Stella as he addressed the girl in the bed.

"Your grandfather will tell you what has been arranged, Francie, my dear," he said quietly, "and I think it will please everyone, except"—for a moment he faced Stella directly, and a faint smile turned up the corners of his sensitive, generous mouth—"it may cause some little inconvenience to your domestic staff to have so many friends of Francie's—friends from the hospital—in and out for a while," he said slowly, "but I assure you this is the only way to please both you and your daughter."

"Whatever it is it's sure to be successful if Father has arranged it," Stella said, and for the life of her Sally could not decide whether she spoke sincerely or with her tongue in her cheek. While she was still trying to make up her mind Curtis spoke again, this time to Sally herself.

"I should like to see you for a few minutes before you go off duty, Staff," he said politely. "It concerns our patient."

Sally thanked him and said she would remember, then the door closed behind him and she was alone with the three members of the Bodman family. Stella was the first to break the silence.

"What have you done, Father?" she asked her father-in-law quietly and still with the little smile playing about her mouth. "Whatever it is you seem pleased with yourself!"

"I am," the old gentleman admitted. "I think I've managed to do what's best for Francie and to please everyone else as well, and that's no mean feat, let me tell you. Francie is going home . . . to Queen's Close . . . to-morrow," he announced in triumph. "Nurse Sally"—he turned to Sally and the bright blue eyes were twinkling— "I'm sorry I don't know your other name, my dear," he apologised, "but that suits you very well, if you will allow an old man to say so, Nurse Sally," he repeated, "is going with you on extended compassionate leave, to look after her friend. The mobile therapy unit will visit twice a week . . . they only do outlying districts as a rule, but they're making an exception in this case, and Mr. Palmer will look in every day so long as he thinks it necessary to do so. Now"—he beamed round on them all—"don't tell me any of you could have managed things any better than that!"

"We couldn't have managed matters half so well, as you know, Father," Stella admitted, "and I must say yours is an even better scheme than mine . . . to have Francie at *home* . . . and to have her taken care of by the person she wants most of all." She turned to Sally and asked, as though there could be no question of refusal, "You will come, won't you, Nurse? We shall make you most comfortable."

"You will, won't you?" Francie insisted from the bed, and Sally nodded, thinking how much she would miss Betty and the others, all the dear, familiar life of the busy hospital, but how much it evidently meant to Francie to have her say 'yes'.

"Of course, if that's all right with Matron," she said simply. "I have to take my orders from her, you know."

"It was Matron's idea." Sam Bodman turned his bright gaze on her, his eyes still twinkling. "And that reminds me," he went on, "you're evidently going to be a very busy girl when you come off duty, Nurse. Matron asked me to tell you she would like to see you in her office for a few minutes before you go across to the nurses' home."

"Thank you." Sally nodded. "I won't forget."

Sam Bodman seated himself on the edge of the bed and took one of his granddaughter's limp hands in his own wrinkled ones. He seemed oblivious of both his daughter-in-law and of Sally as he bent low over the girl in the bed.

"And now, love," he said coaxingly, "tell me what this is all about. I only heard by accident that you were in the Infirmary. Ned Falkingham was over in the States and we ran across each other at a business conference a couple of mornings back. His granddaughter is a cadet nurse here, and it seems she had told him *my* granddaughter had been admitted as a patient, but she didn't know why except that there had been some sort of an accident. I was lucky enough to get a seat on the next flight back, and"—he chuckled in evident satisfaction—"here I am." He patted her hand gently, glancing up at the two pulleys above the bed. "Now, tell me all about it," he invited. "Was it . . . the car?"

"No, Grandpa." Francie's voice was low, and Sally, knowing Matron would have told the old gentleman something of the true outline of the story, found herself praying the girl would not try to hide the truth. She need not have feared on that account. Simply and starkly the girl told the brief story, concluding with the words: "and Sally saw me fall. She didn't hesitate. She couldn't have done, or I'd have been carried on to Wentforth lock. She plunged in and pulled me out. Then, I suppose, she telephoned for the ambulance. When I finally came round, I was here, and Sally was with me. She's been here most of the time ever since."

"Mr. Palmer says you've been very lucky," Sam informed her. "That you could have broken your spine, fractured your skull badly, but that as it is, you'll be walking again in a couple of months, just as well as ever you were. But"—he narrowed his eyes under the bushy eyebrows—"a lot of that is up to you, Francie, isn't it, Nurse?"

"It is," Sally agreed. "And Francie will do it. She's an excellent patient." She smiled. "We'll have her walking—running—playing tennis again before she knows where she is."

"And when you're stronger we'll see what can be done about what it was that worried you so much you had to choose such a silly place to sit and think," Sam said crisply. "Right now, let it wait. Whatever it is it won't spoil."

He rose to his feet as he spoke and held out his hand to Stella.

"We mustn't trespass on good nature or abuse any privileges, my dear," he said firmly. "We ought not to be here at this day and hour, and we must go. Say goodbye to Francie for the present. You and I have a lot to do at Queen's Close before she arrives in the ambulance tomorrow morning."

Stella stooped and kissed her daughter. Whatever her faults, Sally decided, as she saw the look of utter devotion in the mother's eyes, Stella Bodman, and presumably her husband, believed they had always acted in the best interests of their daughter and would not, knowingly or willingly, have caused her distress in any way.

'What a strange thing this love really is,' thought Sally, as she deliberately closed her ears to their conversation. 'Mrs. Bodman loves her daughter, Francie loves her parents, all of them love each other, but they've really caused her more harm than if they had allowed her to run a little wild. Or have they? She's been lucky . . . but she still hasn't found her happiness, and she's still unable to talk to them. She can talk to her grandfather, though, but,' she suppressed a chuckle, 'I suspect he might be tactless enough to offer Martin Howbury a rise or something of that kind, and if I'm any judge of human nature that would be the worst possible thing he could do, unless he had some real and valid reason—apart from Francie's future happiness—for doing it. I shall have to try and talk to the old gentleman about all this. He seems friendly enough and easy to talk to. But I don't know what to suggest either.'

Sam Bodman was propelling his daughter-in-law from the ward, and he stopped *en route* for the door to say *au revoir* to Sally.

"We shall see you tomorrow, Nurse," he said crisply. "I'm more indebted to you than money can ever repay. You don't know what this young lady means to me . . . to all of us."

"I can guess." Sally smiled, and then, greatly daring, she added: "And she's a pretty important person to herself, you know, Mr. Bodman."

The bright blue eyes looked at her with a shrewd glance which told Sally he understood what she was trying to say.

"You mean she has a right to live her own life, don't you, Nurse?" he asked quickly, nodding his head with its ring of silvery fluff round the pink bald patch in the middle. "I couldn't agree more . . . and when you're with us at Queen's Close you and I must get together and see what we can do to help matters along in the right direction. And," he added sharply, placing the responsibility suddenly and squarely upon Sally's shoulders, "I shall look to you to be the one to supply that right direction, Nurse, so do your best not to fail me."

"I will," Sally promised, and smiled as she spoke. Together, she felt, she and Francie's grandfather might yet find the key to happiness for the girl.

When the visitors had left, Francie could talk about nothing but the days which lay ahead for them at Queen's Close. It was very obvious that the girl loved her home dearly, and Sally found herself looking forward to this coming change in her routine, despite the fact that it meant separation from Betty and all her friends at the hospital.

"You once said you were fond of reading, Sally," Francie talked on. "The library at Queen's Close is marvellous. It was started by my great-grandfather and there are books on every subject under the sun. If you like music you'll be 'in' with Mother. She spends hours on the piano, and there's a radiogram, a tape recorder, record player and every kind of music on records or tapes you could wish to hear."

"I'm coming to work, remember," Sally reminded her, laughing. "We have to get you walking as soon as we can . . . then running and playing tennis and all the rest of it, just as you used to do."

"We will," Francie said quickly. "You'll be amazed how much better I'll be once I'm back at Queen's Close, especially if you're there as well."

So, in talk and laughter and in happy anticipation, the time passed quickly by until it was the appointed hour for Sally to go off duty.

"I don't know what time they will arrange for the ambulance to be ready to take you home," she told Francie, on leaving her patient, "but whatever time it is, try to keep your natural excitement down to a minimum. We mustn't have your temperature rising or anything like that happening, or you may not be allowed to go home after all."

"I'll be good," Francie promised, "and I shall sleep like a top tonight—without any sedative tablets—and be ready before you even reach me tomorrow. You just wait and see!"

Sally, laughing, had almost reached the door when Francie called her back.

"There's just one point," she said in a very small voice. "I don't suppose it's likely, but one never knows, and I keep hoping . . . supposing Martin decided that after all he would like to see for himself how I am? There's a long visiting time tomorrow, and the *Chronicle* comes out for the week in the morning, so he won't be quite so pushed as he is the days before it's printed . . . what if he comes and I'm not here? He'd feel an awful fool, and he wouldn't think any better of me for letting him come right out here for nothing."

"What do you want me to do?" Sally asked patiently. "I could try and telephone him, now I'm off duty."

"You couldn't—it's too much to ask, I suppose, but if you could go into Barcaster and see him," Francie began half hopefully, "you could *tell* him how much I loved his flowers, how grateful I am, but how disappointed by his message. If you telephoned, you see, he could put you off, make it so that you had to leave a message, and you couldn't say all that sort of thing in a message you had to leave with someone else."

"No," Sally admitted doubtfully, "I couldn't. But"— she glanced at her watch—"I have to see Mr. Palmer, and Matron, too, and by the time I'm through with them I should think your Martin will have gone home to wherever he lives for some well-earned rest."

"Not tonight he won't," Francie said quickly. "I told you, they do what they call 'putting the paper to bed' tonight, that means it's printed during the evening and the early hours of the night and ready for sale in the morning. Martin never goes home early, not any night, but Wednesdays are his latest nights of all, just because of this. I don't know why, but they put out a night paper every night and it doesn't seem to occasion half so much fuss."

"They'll have their reasons, no doubt," Sally said crisply. "In that case," she added a little doubtfully, not particularly relishing her errand, "I'll try and get over to see him for you. But I must see Mr. Palmer and Matron first."

"There'll still be plenty of time," Francie said contentedly. "Now I can settle down."

But if Francie could 'settle down' feeling everything was under control, Sally found the same could scarcely be said of herself. She went first to the wash-room and made certain she was as spick and span as was humanly possible before she went demurely along the corridor in search of Curtis. She found him in the consultants' sitting-room, enjoying a cup of tea, and as soon as she appeared he insisted that she join him.

"You've been working under considerable strain, Nurse," he surprised Sally by saying. "I know. I've worked for the Bodman family before today, and we were up against the same sort of thing with Miss Bodman's mother then as we are this time. She is a charming woman —they are a charming and delightful family—not the least of their charms being the work they all do for this hospital and the large amounts of money they are always willing to give to make certain it remains the best-equipped hospital in the Midlands. But"—the grey-blue eyes twinkled suddenly and the generous mouth quirked upwards at the corners—"Mrs. Bodman junior doesn't appear to realise or accept that any institution such as this must have rules and regulations, and that these are there to be obeyed."

"I suppose," Sally began doubtfully as he paused, evidently waiting for her to speak, "she is used to *issuing* the orders, not accepting them. It must be difficult for her to realise that there are times when authority has to make the decisions."

"That's the point," Curtis nodded agreement. "I couldn't have put it better myself, and the fact that you realise this makes what I have to say easier. I know Matron will be talking to you and that you take your orders as a nurse from her, but I am in charge of Miss Bodman's case, and I feel I have a right to say something which I consider may be of help to you as her nurse."

Sally waited a moment or so and, after a brief pause in which he was evidently choosing his words, he went on:

"Here you have set hours," he said slowly. "I know that at times those hours are longer than they should be—when we have an emergency, as an example. But that time is always made up to you. Here you have set free time. Free days. Here the ward maids do a great deal of the work which is concerned with the care of the patient but is not actual nursing. What I'm trying to say to you, Nurse Nesbitt, is for your own good. With every good intention in the world, Mrs. Bodman will make use of you without even knowing why, and I want to warn you, to tell you that, for your own sake, you must see such a thing doesn't happen."

"You're . . . very kind," Sally managed at last, wondering why he should be taking all this trouble when both of them knew Matron would have a few words to say on how Sally should conduct herself on her new case. "I'll remember all you have said," she promised.

Curtis smiled and rose, glancing at his watch so that she knew he must be due elsewhere in the hospital and it was time she should be leaving him.

"Do," he said soberly, then the slow smile came, transforming his rather stern features. "I'm only thinking of *you*," he stressed. "You are unsparing of yourself—most of the nurses here are, I know, in fact nurses everywhere —but you've already risked your life for this patient, and nursed her devotedly ever since. In addition"—he held open the door for Sally—"it hasn't escaped my notice that Miss Bodman is . . . making use of you in other ways . . . perhaps to further some love affair, to follow some bent of her own which may or may not meet with her family's approval and could thus call down their anger on your unsuspecting head."

"It's nothing like that." In spite of her respect for him both as a man in his position at the hospital, Sally felt she must register a protest on Francie's behalf. "I . . . I promised to take a message for her tonight," she rushed on, aware that the tell-tale colour was staining her cheeks and, apparently, amusing Curtis. "She hasn't anyone else she can ask," she ended lamely.

"I suppose not," he said sharply. "Most people in her position would find the same thing . . . there are few people they *can* trust, which makes their friendship rather hard on those few." Abruptly his mood changed and he laid one hand on her shoulder in a comforting, brotherly gesture. "Don't worry about it," he said in a more gentle tone. "Just remember to take care of yourself and not to allow them to put upon you . . . Mrs. Bodman in particular."

"I'll remember," Sally promised, and went on her way to Matron's office, a comforting glow inexplicably settling round her heart.

Matron was busily engaged with some papers on her desk when she called Sally to come in, but in a few moments she had pushed these on one side and smiled at the girl whom she had gestured to a chair facing her.

"You will know of the arrangements that have been made with regard to Miss Bodman, Staff?" she queried. "I take it you have no objections to them in any way?"

"No, Matron, thank you," Sally assured her. "I'm proud Miss Bodman asked for me . . . I shall do my best for her, as you know."

"I know you will." Matron nodded, folded her arms on the desk and rested her chin on her upheld palms. "I don't need to tell you how important the Bodman family are in Barcaster," she said simply. "Here, as you know, whoever enters for treatment is equally important, but that does not alter the fact that Samuel Bodman has, over the past ten years or so, since he has been Chairman of the Committee, donated thousands of pounds' worth of equipment to the General and is, I understand, likely to donate much more."

"I know that he has been very generous," Sally murmured as Matron paused.

"And will continue so to be," Matron spoke solemnly. "I feel sure, just as he has now extended a welcome—and a genuine one—to any of your friends from here who may wish to visit you in your off-duty periods. Mr. Palmer," she frowned slightly and continued, "will, of course, be visiting Miss Bodman . . . how frequently I cannot say, but her grandfather has made it plain that he and others are to be made most welcome at Queen's Close. Now, Nurse, I'm not even suggesting that you don't know how to conduct yourself no matter what the circumstances, but Mr. Palmer has great hopes from Mr. Bodman regarding some very expensive equipment which he would like in the theatre. I am not unaware"—a faint smile touched her firm lips—"that a number of my nurses have a certain special regard for Mr. Palmer. I'm not suggesting you are one of that number. I'm merely reminding you—asking you to remember—that Mr. Palmer will be calling frequently at Queen's Close, but that he is there to visit a patient, Miss Bodman, and that is the reason for his visits."

Sally felt the colour rise to her cheeks at Matron's implication, but years of training stood her in good stead and, not betraying by one flicker of an eyelash the tremendous tumult Matron's words had aroused in her, she answered steadily, her voice quite under control.

"I'm not likely to forget, Matron. My free time will, I suppose, mostly be spent in Barcaster with Michael Amberton. He's a reporter with the *Chronicle*."

"I see." She could tell nothing of what Matron thought of the information by either her expression or the tone of her voice, but the interview was apparently over, for, her warning delivered, it did not take Matron long to wish her well in this new phase and to say how delighted she was that Sally had apparently pleased the Bodman family so much so far.

Out in the corridor Sally clenched her hands until the knuckles showed white.

'First *he* warns me about Mrs. Bodman, then Matron warns me against reading something personal into his visits! The sooner this job is over and Francie walking about again and I'm back at the General the better I'll be pleased! I almost wish I hadn't said I would go to see Martin for her.' But a sudden mental picture of Francie's lovely little face, wistful and lonely, softened her heart.

'She's been up against this sort of thing in different ways all her life,' she remembered. 'Well, I'm not used to anyone telling me how to conduct myself. I'll just go on as I always have done, and if it doesn't work out right, then will be the time to worry. But I'm not worrying *now* . . .' With which resolve she marched firmly out of the hospital and over to the nurses' home to prepare for her second visit to Martin Howbury.

CHAPTER TEN

SALLY felt it would take her most of the journey into Barcaster to recover from the two interviews she had just experienced. Taking her usual seat at the front of the top deck of the bus, Sally lit a cigarette and tried to relax. It would never do for her to look for Martin Howbury— and find him—while in this mood. She might feel inclined to say something she ought not to say—something she had no right to say—but which might give him a push in the direction of Francie Bodman . . . or send him away altogether!

She descended from the bus at the crossroads, one of which led through the town to the offices of the *Chronicle*. Coming towards her along the street, braking as she hesitated at the zebra crossing, was a bright blue mini, the driver of which smiled and nodded at Sally in a most friendly manner, waving her to proceed and beaming in unmistakable friendliness. For a moment Sally could not recall the fact, that of a middle-aged woman, skilfully but not obviously made-up, the crown of silvered hair, elegantly dressed, the general air of knowing her person-ally. Then the woman turned her head, still smiling, and Sally knew where she had seen her before.

'Mrs Curtis Anderby Palmer!' she breathed to herself. '*His* mother. She remembered seeing me at the flower show . . .' and for no reason at all she felt suddenly cheered by the thought that Curtis's mother had seen and remembered her, although they had not been formally introduced.

'I wonder what Matron would make of that!' Sally smiled as she turned into the doorway of the *Chronicle* building. 'She couldn't say I was reading anything but friendliness into such a chance encounter . . . or that anything else was meant,' with which illogical reasoning she rattled furiously on the locked doors of the newspaper building, but all to no avail.

"If it's something important you want I should go round the back. They're still working, but they won't hear you with the press going and nobody in the offices at this time."

Sally glanced round. A small elderly man was sitting on an old stool in the shelter of a doorway farther down. Before him stood a flat hand-cart arrangement piled high with evening papers and a small tin tray of money.

"They work late tonight." He was prepared to talk if Sally would listen. "*Chronicle*'s out in the morning, you see. If it's something for this week's paper you're too late, but if it's for tomorrow evening's you'll be all right. And if it's personal, like," he ended, evidently consumed by curiosity, "it depends who it is you want to see."

"I want to see Mr. Howbury, the editor," Sally said, wondering if she had done the wrong thing in telling this man even a little of her business, but evidently his curiosity was now satisfied.

"Oh, he'll still be there." The old man extracted a red spotted handkerchief from his pocket and blew his nose vigorously. "Always the last to go, is our Martin," he observed. "Turn left round the end of the building here, then down the little passage on your right. Press room— printing room—whatever they call it, it's there. Big green door facing you. You'll most likely find Mr. Howbury in there."

"Thank you," Sally managed, and turned to follow his directions.

She could hear the press long before she reached the big green door. For a moment she stood listening, and an unidentified phrase, a snatch of something learned long ago, returned to her mind to tease her.

'The thunder and the power of the press . . .' Sally did not know where she had read the words, but their force struck her with renewed understanding as she listened to the machines thundering out the news, the announcements of birth and death and marriage, of gossip and fact, all the little things which added together made up the sum of the press of a fairly important and thriving town. As she stood there, listening and wondering for a moment what it was like to work on such a paper, the big green door opened and Martin Howbury was coming towards her. He had not seen her, and was almost level when Sally caught at his sleeve.

"Mr. Howbury," she began premonitorily. "Just a moment, please."

He looked down at her, and at first glance, Sally knew, he did not recognise her. He looked tired, his hair was still awry, and his tie was out of position. Perhaps it was her imagination, Sally told herself, but he looked strained, a little thinner about the face than when she had last seen him. For a blank moment he stared at her and then she saw the recognition light his eyes.

"Why, if it isn't the little staff nurse from up at the General Hospital!" he exclaimed. "Nurse . . . Nesbitt, isn't it?" He peered more closely at her, and Sally saw how tired his eyes looked. "There's nothing wrong, is there, Nurse?" he enquired, sudden anxiety reaching his tone. "Not more than there was . . . with . . . Francie, I mean?"

"No." Sally could never bear to keep anyone in suspense and she hastened now to allay his fears. "Francie is much improved," she told him truthfully. "She asked me to come and tell you she's going home tomorrow, back to Queen's Close."

"Then she's really better?" There was a note of accusation in his voice as he continued. "I'm glad," he said sincerely, "but I don't think, if that's the case, she could have been anything like so badly hurt as you made out to me, Nurse," he ended.

"She's not better." Sally stressed the 'not'. "She's going home because everyone—her grandfather, her mother, Matron—everyone thinks it would be better for her to be in familiar surroundings." She did not think it tactful to say that Mrs. Bodman had wanted to remove her daughter to The Mount so that she could visit when she liked, but it seemed Martin knew Francie's mother well enough to guess what had happened.

"There must be some arrangement for someone to give her proper care," he said quietly. "Even Stella Bodman must know that is more important than having her own way, sweetly as she usually manages to achieve it."

Sally could not help a little smile. He had hit the nail on the head without any help from her!

"It all depends," she said slowly, "just what you mean by 'proper care', doesn't it, Mr. Howbury? I'm going with Miss Bodman . . . on extended compassionate leave," she quoted Samuel Bodman's words carefully, "and Mr. Palmer—the surgeon—will look in on her perhaps every day until he's certain all is well. The physiotherapy people are calling with their mobile unit——"

"I get it," Martin interrupted. "You don't have to say any more. All the benefits of the hospital plus all the comforts of home, possible only if you have a grandfather like old Samuel. Don't misunderstand me." He held up his hand, as it was obvious Sally was about to speak. "I think he's the finest man in the world, and who can blame him if he looks after his own? I only wish——" He broke off, looking intently at Sally. "Did she get my flowers?" he asked unexpectedly. "And could she . . . read the message?"

"She received them and she loved them," Sally told him quietly, "but can you blame her if she was hurt and disappointed when she found out their meanings?"

"It's the best way," Martin said doggedly. "She'll know one day that what I've done was . . . for her."

"She knows that," Sally answered him simply, "but she doesn't agree it's for the best." She remembered suddenly that Francie had said she would find a way to make Martin change his mind, that she would never give him up, and, emboldened by the memory, she made herself ask again: "Won't you come to the house and see her? I know both Francie and her mother, and her grandfather, too, have said they would welcome any of her friends."

"I often go there," Martin said, "but I shan't be going again for some time. I'm fond of the old gentleman, as I told you. He has done a lot for me, and I serve him to the best of my ability, but this makes a difference."

"I only came," Sally turned away, "because Francie thought you might . . . change your mind and go to see her at the hospital. She didn't want you to trail out there and then find her gone."

"That was thoughtful, and typical of Francie," Martin told her, "but she doesn't see what's best for herself, and I do. Thank her for letting me know she was going home. Tell her I hope she'll soon be well, but don't," he added so sharply that Sally jumped, "encourage her to think I shall be coming to see her. I shan't do that," he said firmly, "unless I know she is really in need of me. Maybe, in a year or two, when she's had time to forget me, then we'll meet again. A lot of water can run under the bridge in two or three years. We both may have different ideas by that time. At least, we'll wait and see."

"I'll tell her." Sally turned away and began to walk back down the corridor, but before she reached its end Martin had called her back to him.

"Tell her if ever she really needs me, then I'll come," he said with obvious reluctance. "And tell her also that if she does find someone else as I'm sure she will and I hope she will, someone with whom she can be really happy—that I shall think it an honour to be the first to know. There wouldn't be any point in dreaming of that mythical best-seller or film story then," he ended with a touch of bitterness which Sally found unexpectedly touching. "Thank you for coming," Martin ended suddenly. "I'm glad she has you for a friend, Sally. Let me know how things go with her, will you?" Then she was hurrying along the passageway and out into the little back road which ran round the printing works.

"Sorry . . . whoops! Sally! What in the name of all

that's wonderful are you doing here at this hour?" She found herself caught and held in Mike's strong arms, and for one brief moment they stood, close together, then Sally laughed and moved away.

"I might ask you the same thing," she teased. "When you telephoned this morning you said you'd be working late tonight, but I thought you were a reporter, not a compositor or whatever is the correct term."

"I've been out with the photographers," Mike explained. "But that doesn't tell me why you're here. Nothing wrong, is there?" he added anxiously.

"No." Sally shook her head. "Just that Francie wanted Mr. Howbury to know she's going home tomorrow, and he doesn't want to do anything about it."

"He has his pride." Mike took her arm. "I think he's wrong, because they're made for each other, but I can understand his point of view. Come along to the Copper Bowl," he invited. "We can have a bite of supper and I'll run you back. It'll be just as quick as if you waited for the bus. I promise"—he grinned—"I won't ask you to marry me, not tonight. Unless"—the grin widened—"you might have changed your mind since I saw you last. Any chance?"

"Sorry," Sally smiled, but she meant that 'sorry'. Mike was the nicest person she knew, she reflected. He took her hand firmly in his own and tucked it securely under his arm.

"I can wait," he said quietly as he had said so often, "until I know it's hopeless. But I warn you, if some wealthy heiress comes along, beautiful as you and just as charming and who doesn't express revulsion in my direction, I might be tempted to change my mind! But as that isn't likely, come and eat and put me up to date with all your news."

As always Sally was relaxed and happy with Mike. They had a salad supper, coffee and biscuits, then Mike glanced at his watch and decided it was time to take her back to the nurses' home.

"I'm telling you," he said as he tucked her into his little car, "that if by any chance I get an invitation out to Queen's Close I shall be there as fast and as soon as this little old jalopy can make it. I'd like to see the place at close quarters." He laughed. "I've been twice, to functions the old man had there for the staff, but they weren't behaving like folks at home then. They were staff occasions, very formal and all that sort of thing. I'd really like to see for myself, when all the office aren't there, if you know what I mean. Not to mention," he steered round a difficult corner not looking at her, "the fact that I shall keep an eye on you, even though you're going places, or so it seems."

"I'm not," Sally protested. "I'm just doing my own job . . . but in different surroundings. That's all. There's no more to it than that."

"There may be," Mike said darkly. "Things have a habit of going forward, once the wheels are set in motion. People start something with the best intentions in the world, and before you know it whatever it is they've started has taken on a sort of life of its own and moved farther than they intended or in a different direction. I've a funny feeling about this job, Sally," he said with more than a serious note in his voice. "I've a feeling it's going to mean something special to us . . . to you and to me . . . but whether that something special is going to be good or bad I just don't know."

He sounded so serious, so unlike the Mike she knew so well, that Sally turned to look at him, wondering what was wrong. He must have sensed her glance, for he turned to look at her, taking his gaze from the road for a moment or two.

"Don't look so worried, love," he counselled. "Even if this feeling . . . premonition or whatever it is . . . means you're going to find someone else while you're at Queen's Close and that's the end of a dream for me, it won't change what I feel for you, it won't change the fact that, come what may, I'll always be the same old reliable, dependable Mike, around if you want me and willing to disappear if you don't. But until whatever it is that's to happen *does* happen, don't let it worry you. I'm always like this when I've been out with the photographers," he laughed as he explained. "It must be some sort of reaction. We went to photograph an accident," he told her. "Even when I'm objective about these things they still do something to me . . . ever since I met you. It didn't matter before. You're sure you won't change your mind?" he asked still seriously. "About me, I mean. I'm not repulsive to you, that's obvious, and you say there isn't anyone else . . ."

"There isn't," Sally insisted, adding cautiously and truthfully, "not in the way you mean."

"Then there is someone, but . . . what is it, Sally? Is he married or something?"

"No," Sally laughed a little, but there was pain behind the laughter. "He's not married," she told him. "He . . . just doesn't see my sex, that's all."

"I'm not with you." Mike pulled the car to the side of the road and switched off the engine and Sally saw to her amazement they were almost at the entrance to the driveway to the nurses' home. "I don't understand," he said, "but I gather there *is* someone, who, because he's blind or something, doesn't know you . . . care. That's it, isn't it, Sally? Do I know him?"

"No." Sally shook her head. "I'm sure you don't. And it doesn't matter," she went on brightly, opening the door and getting out into the road. "Like you said a moment ago . . . it's just a dream. And we all have to wake up from dreaming some time." She smiled at him in the dim light, thinking how strange it was that she could always talk to Mike in this way and know he would understand. "It needn't make any difference to us, unless you want it to, that is, unless you want to stop seeing me," she said a little unsteadily.

"It won't make any difference to me," he assured her, reaching out and laying a hand on hers where it rested on the car door. "Not until you tell me you've found what you wanted . . . then I'll leave you to it." He looked up again and the old, happy grin was back. "I'm a hard-bitten newspaper man," he reminded her. "No need to break your heart over me, love. I shall go on . . . hoping. Until I know there's no hope left. Then I'll quit, but I shan't grizzle . . . and I'll still be there if you need me."

D

Sally felt her eyes mist over with tears, but no words would come. She gave his fingers a quick squeeze and then turned, calling a choked 'goodnight' as she went, running down the path to the home before she broke down and the tears spilled over.

Betty was already in bed, reading, but she looked up as Sally entered, her welcoming smile fading as she saw the other girl's face.

"What's wrong, Sally?" she asked, laying her book on one side. "You look upset."

"I am." Sally sniffed, wiped her nose and laughed a little at herself. "It's Mike," she gave the disjointed explanation. "Why can't I love him, Betty? He's everything any girl ought to want, and he'll do anything in the world for me . . ."

"Except stop loving you, and he can't do that." Betty sat up, prepared to talk. "It's something you can't change, Sally," she said slowly. "It's either there or it's not. I used to think it was as easy to love one man as the next . . . I've said so to you, often. Now I know better. Pete's the man for me. He'll always have woman trouble. He can't help it. When he goes into practice with his father as he hopes to be able to do it'll be up to me to keep him out of trouble . . . trouble he invites without knowing how or why he does it. But I couldn't love anyone else the way I love him, even though I know there'll be times when I wish I'd never seen him."

She was silent a moment, but as Sally made no answer she went on, talking as much to herself as the other girl.

"I used to think you were a sentimental ass," she said unexpectedly. "You always said marriage without love was cheating. You're right, Sally, and if all you can feel for Mike is a sisterly love, then hang on. Don't give way and marry him because you think you should if he loves you so much. Believe me, I know now that you'd regret it in the end."

"But it doesn't seem fair," Sally protested at length. "He takes me out. He's willing to go anywhere, do anything I ask. He's always thinking of me . . ."

"And you're always thinking of Curtis Palmer," Betty finished for her. "Come on, now, admit it!"

For a moment Sally was silent, then in the face of those clear green eyes watching her so intently and with such loving concern, she knew it would be impossible to prevaricate.

"And if I am?" she began defensively. "A cat may look at a king, or so they say."

"With what result, who can say?" Betty countered teasingly. "We all know how often he's been in to see Miss Bodman, but who is to say it was not Miss Bodman's nurse he wanted to see instead?" She sank down in bed, yawning. "More unlikely things have happened, both in and out of hospitals," she said sleepily. "But I shouldn't count on anything if I were you, Sally. Just keep your fingers crossed, and I'll do the same for you. See you in the morning before you go . . . and heaven knows, I'm going to miss you!"

CHAPTER ELEVEN

As the ambulance rolled away from the General Hospital early the following morning, Sally could not help but think of Betty's words, 'Heaven knows, I'm going to miss you!'

'I'm going to miss her, too,' she thought, glancing out of the window as the vehicle passed through the hospital gates. 'I'm going to miss all this—all the people about the hospital, the routine, everything and everyone. It's all going to be so very different, and I'm not in the least bit sure I'm going to like it. I don't think I'd like to go private nursing all the time . . . I thought so once, but now I'm not sure.'

"Sally!" Francie, prone on the stretcher bed in the ambulance, called at that moment, and Sally turned instantly to see what she wanted.

"Comfy?" she asked lightly, straightening the blanket

almost automatically. "Not a very smooth ride, I'm afraid."

"It's not that." For a moment Francie's violet blue eyes looked into Sally's with a clear, searching gaze as she asked: "You're sure you don't mind? All this change, I mean. I could just as well have stayed at the hospital without all this upheaval for you, if only Mummy would see that rules and regulations are really there to help people, not just to annoy them."

"I don't mind," Sally said promptly, dismissing all thoughts of Betty, her friendships with the other nurses, the regular routine of her hospital life. "I shall enjoy the change. It will be good for me. It isn't a good thing for anyone to get into a rut, and it was time I had a change of some sort."

She scarcely listened as Francie went on talking. Her own words had conjured up something else in her mind, a picture of Mike on the previous evening, when he had asked her if there was 'someone else'. Perhaps going around with Mike for so long, as she had done, liking but not loving him, was a habit with them both . . . a routine . . . even a rut. Perhaps it was something she ought to have broken off before now as being unfair to Mike, since it was fairly obvious he would never voluntarily break their friendship himself.

'But if I suggest it he says he's quite contented and happy to go on as we are,' she reflected. 'And, goodness knows, I'd miss Mike and his friendship, just as I know I'm going to miss being at the General.'

"Here we are," Francie suddenly announced. "I can tell by the tree-tops."

Sally looked out of the window and saw they were passing along an avenue lined with poplar trees, their tops waving in the breeze way above the roof of the vehicle.

"Quite a landmark," she observed. "I've noticed them from the roadway. They look most effective."

"They are," Francie confirmed the statement. "And they're friendly trees. I used to talk to them when I was a little girl."

Sally choked back the words she had been about to say

as she thought of a child so lonely that she had to find companionship among the trees.

"You must love them very much," was all she said, and at that moment the ambulance rounded the last curve of the drive and came to a halt at the foot of a flight of wide stone steps leading to the huge oak door which stood wide open, with Francie's parents and her grandfather waiting to welcome her home.

Sally supervised the lifting of her patient from the ambulance, and the carrying up the steps to the low but light room on the ground floor which had been made ready for her.

"I put you in here, dear, and Nurse next door, for the time being," her mother was saying as she led the way. "You see, Mr. Palmer said it would not be long before you were able to walk and also that you would have to exercise. We thought the terrace would be the ideal spot, and that if you were downstairs already you wouldn't have the trouble—both for you and for Nurse—of negotiating the stairway every day."

"Very thoughtful." Sally looked round approvingly and could find no fault. "This should be ideal."

The ground floor of this wing of the house had, it appeared, been transformed to accommodate Francie and Sally for as long as it should be necessary. Sally stifled a sigh as she thought of what work and expense must have been involved. Only someone who had as much money to spare as the Bodman family could have achieved so much in such a short space of time and without there being any evidence of upheaval.

'No wonder Martin thinks he'll never make enough money to compensate for taking her away from all this,' Sally thought. 'But money isn't everything, and I'm sure Francie would rather have less *and* Martin than all this and talk to trees!'

She knew she was being a little absurd, for it was perfectly obvious that Francie no longer found it necessary to seek companionship in such a fashion, but all the same the picture of a lonely child, a self-contained girl— a girl driven back in on herself—remained.

"We'll leave you to get settled in." Robert Bodman took his wife firmly by the arm and began to lead her from the room. "Francie looks so much better that we must be careful not to upset her by giving her too much excitement. If you approve, Nurse," he added as he also shepherded his father before him, "we'll all come along for a chat after lunch, when Francie has had a rest. Father has a surprise for you then, I think."

"Indeed I have, yes, indeed." Sam gave a little chuckle and beamed upon Sally. "Two surprises, in fact," he admitted. "We'll see you after luncheon, Nurse, and I hope you'll like what I have in store for you."

"I'm sure I shall," Sally said rashly. "Thank you very much."

"Wait and see first," the old gentleman laughed. "I may have made a mistake after all, but I hope not. I was acting under advice in one case," he admitted.

Quite intrigued, despite herself, Sally scarcely heard Stella Bodman explaining that Ivy, who had been with the family for years, would be looking after Sally and her charge personally.

"If there is anything you especially like, Nurse," Stella concluded, "I do hope you will say so. I appreciate your coming here to care for Francie. No"—she smiled and held up her hand as Sally began to speak—"don't tell me you're doing your duty and that this is all Matron's doing. You could have refused to come if you had so chosen, and then the improvement in Francie's condition would have stopped when your attention ceased. I know my daughter"—she smiled fondly at the girl—"and she hasn't made many friends—not even among the families of our own friends—and when once she takes to anyone that person can do no wrong. I always say"—she laughed a little—"that when she falls in love I pray it will be with someone of whom we can approve, someone we can all like, because she'll never change, not once her heart is given.

"You must come along, my dear, and leave Nurse to settle Francie down or whatever it is she has to do at this stage." Robert smiled at Sally. It was plain that he adored his wife, but felt at times it was necessary to control her extravagances, both emotional and otherwise, just a little. "You can talk all you wish later."

"I just wanted Nurse to know how much we appreciate her coming here, saving Francie's life in the beginning and . . . everything," she managed a final word. "I don't forget"—she delicately repressed a shudder—"that if it hadn't been for Nurse Sally's prompt and courageous action we might never have seen Francie again . . . alive."

"None of us are likely to forget that, my dear," Robert assured her, "and the best way we can show our appreciation is to co-operate all we can right now." He turned to Sally as he left the room. "What we would like to make clear," he said simply, "is that we wish to show our gratitude in a practical way, first by making sure of your every comfort while you are with us. If the bed isn't comfortable, if the food is not what you like or are accustomed to, please don't hesitate to say so, will you, Nurse? Remember, we owe you a great deal, and whatever you ask will be small repayment."

"I'm sure everything will be simply wonderful," Sally told them all, her eyes shining at the kindliness of their welcome, sure now that she would be completely at ease with them all. "Thank you."

They left then, evidently satisfied that Francie was once more safely under her own roof and in good hands, and by the time Sally had her charge settled comfortably, her personal things distributed about the three rooms which had been made ready for their use, there came a quiet double knock on the door.

"Come in, Ivy," Francie called, before Sally had quite realised what was happening, and a moment later the tall, well-built figure of a young woman about twenty-eight or nine entered, pushing a dumb waiter.

"I'm glad to see you again, Ivy," Francie said quickly. "Is . . . everything all right now?" she asked, waving her left hand.

"Yes, thank you, Miss Francie." The girl held out her hand and Sally saw the gleam of a modest little ring on the third finger. "I don't wear it when I'm working, not really," she went on, "but I knew you'd want to see. We're going to be married in September, and your grandfather says there'll be one of the estate cottages ready by then, so I can keep on here helping every day, and Ned will of course still be in the gardens. It's all worked out right after all," she ended with a sigh of satisfaction.

"I'm so glad." Francie's words and tone were quite sincere, but Sally's trained, quick ear caught the undernote of resignation and she knew the girl was thinking of Martin and wondering why things did not 'work out right' for her as well. The moment of slight depression was gone so quickly that Sally would have sworn Ivy had not even noted it, and a moment later Francie was introducing the maid to the nurse.

"It was Nurse Sally who saved my life," she concluded, "and now she's come home with me to make certain I do all the things I should and"—she grinned mischievously—"none of the things I should *not* do, and get well as quickly as possible."

"We'll do our best in the kitchen," Ivy smiled, eyeing them both, "but I can't say either of you looks in need of feeding up or anything like that."

"Just good, plain food at regular times," Sally laughed. "That's what I'm accustomed to. Though I shan't mind being spoiled for a little just by way of a change," she added, as the tempting odour of roast duckling filled the air.

"If there's anything you especially fancy, Nurse, Mrs. Bodman says you're to tell me the night before, please," Ivy requested. "She makes up the menus for the day first thing every morning, along with Cook, you see."

"I'm sure everything will be perfect, Ivy"—Sally smiled—"and I thank you all very much."

"It's a pleasure," Ivy said sincerely. "The place hasn't been the same without Miss Francie, and to think that but for you she might have gone for ever!" she finished dramatically.

"Someone else would have seen her." Sally did not intend to allow anyone to emphasise too much what might have happened. When she was overtired Francie was still a little inclined to suffer from nightmares in which her fall from the bridge largely figured. "Anyhow," she brought an end to the conversation by lifting the covers off the dishes and beginning to serve Francie, "all's well that ends well," she quoted, and, nodding in complete agreement, Ivy left them.

The meal was delicious. The roast duckling was accompanied by fresh, new green peas and tiny white potatoes, decorated with mint and parsley. There was a sauce which was both fragrant and piquant, but to which Sally could give no name. To follow there was an iced cherry and pear 'concoction', as Francie styled it, with creamy icecream, and the whole followed by the most delicious coffee Sally had ever tasted. Tea-lover though she might be, this was one occasion when she refilled her cup of something for which she seldom had very much enthusiasm.

"Now sit back and have your cigarette, Sally," Francie said, watching her through half-closed eyes. "Was that meal all right for you?" she ended anxiously.

"It was delicious," Sally said truthfully. "There's only one trouble, if your people are going to treat me like this every day I shall have to organise a five-mile walk every day to take off any extra inches!"

"And you'll have to stay until I can walk those five miles with you," Francie teased. "But I'm glad everything was what you liked, Sally. You've done so much for me."

"No more than my duty," Sally said quickly, but before she could say any more the door opened and Stella and Robert Bodman had returned. They were followed by Ivy, who smiled round at them all—thereby assuring Sally that good relations were evident between the staff and the family—before wheeling the remains of the meal from the room.

"Father will be along in a moment, Nurse." Stella, as usual, opened the conversation. "We didn't think you would be giving Francie any massage or treatment straight away after her meal, so we thought it would be all right if we came along now for a little chat and let you have a rest and a look round first."

"You're very kind," Sally began doubtfully, then as she caught sight of the twinkle in Robert's eyes she smiled at them both. "Very well," she said agreeably, "but please call me if you think there's the slightest need. I do not think there will be. Normally Francie has a little rest herself right now, but I think today she's too excited, and maybe we'll get a good night's rest—and an early one—without resorting to any kind of sedation."

"I hope so." Stella nodded. "Matron tells me you're qualified to give her the necessary massage in between the visits of the mobile therapy people?"

"I took a course," Sally told them, "for cases such as this one."

"But not essential to your qualifications?" Robert asked. "Why?"

"Because there's so much to learn," Sally said quietly and simply. "There are so many ways now to help people, I think we should all know something about as many of them as we possibly can."

"I couldn't agree more," Robert nodded, "but how many of us bother? Not only in your profession," he added more to himself than to the others, "but in every walk of life. Things would be much easier and better all round for a number of others if more of us thought along those lines."

Before Sally had time to say she did this sort of thing because she was fond of her work and glad to know more about every aspect of it, Samuel Bodman had followed his son and daughter-in-law into the room. His bright blue eyes were twinkling, and there was a mischievous smile on his lips.

"Surprise number one, Nurse Sally," he said, extending a small slender box. "I do hope you'll like it. Matron wouldn't hear of my presenting you with Savings Certificates or Premium Bonds or anything like that." He bent forward anxiously as Sally fumbled with the catch. "Let me," he suggested, almost as impatient as a child might have been in like circumstances. "There!" He stood back, a moment or so later, the top of the little box in his hand. "How do you like that?" he questioned.

Sally bent her head and looked into the box to find, resting on its bed of cotton-wool, a tiny wristwatch, jewelled and obviously very expensive, and with a slim gold bracelet adjustable to her wrist.

"I've had it inscribed," Sam said, watching her. "We can, I think, do something about the inscription if you don't like it."

Sally turned the exquisite thing over in her hands and read: "For Sally, with sincere gratitude from the Bodman family," and the date of her dive to the rescue. She looked at the old gentleman, her eyes shining, her lower lip trembling a little.

"It's beautiful," she said sincerely. "But you ought not to have done this. I never thought of any reward . . ."

"We know, we know," Sam said quickly, shaking his head and smiling at her. "But so many people would have seen what was happening and done precisely nothing, nothing that could have done any good, anyway, or not until it was too late. You'll tell me next you were 'only doing your duty', but the fact remains that you did what needed to be done, and did it successfully." He patted her arm in a friendly, fatherly fashion. "Now, my dear," he went on, "let me fasten it on your wrist for you, and then let's go and see my second surprise. I hope it will please you as much as I hope the first one has done."

"It has—I mean—I love the watch," Sally told him quickly. "It's just that it seems too good to wear . . ."

"It's far too 'good', as you put it, to be locked away in a drawer somewhere," old Sam chuckled, "so if I were you I'd wear it whenever you can. And now"—he took her by the arm and led her from the room—"let's go and see the other surprise, then I can come back and have a little chat with Francie before you shoo us all away."

Sally followed him through the suite of rooms which had been made over for her use and Francie's, across the wide hall and into the other wing. At the door of what she found later was known as the second sitting-room, he paused before flinging it open.

"We didn't want you to feel cut off from your friends while you're here, Nurse," he said quietly. "I know

Matron prides herself that the nurses' home really *is* a home, and that is what we wish you to feel of Queen's Close. I'm telling you now," and there was an odd dignity about him suddenly, "that you are at liberty to invite your friends here during your free time while you are under my roof. You're not to feel that because you've come out on this case you're not able to enjoy life as you do with your regulated free time, friendships and all else at the General. If there is anything else you can think of which may add to your sense of comfort and well-being, tell one of us as soon as you can and we'll do all we can to help. And now," still smiling he opened the door of the room and stood on one side to permit her to enter, "have a happy hour or two with your friend," he advised. "Ivy will bring you tea, and we'll all leave Francie when you think it wise."

Sally walked into the room expecting to see Betty awaiting her, but the person who rose from the low arm-chair by the window was not Betty, however, but Mike, his hair on end as usual, his smile in full evidence.

"I don't know how this came about, but I like it," he began, as he saw her embarrassment mingled with the pleasure she always felt whenever she met Mike. "The boss just rang through to my desk and asked if I was a friend of yours, and when I said 'yes' he said 'That's all right, then, you must be the one Mr. Samuel means,' so here I am. I don't know what it's all about, since it's obvious you didn't send for me . . . or did you?" he asked, on a sudden note of hope, but Sally, pulling out a chair to place beside his before he could reach one for her, shook her head.

"No," she said regretfully, "I didn't send for you, Mike. But it's nice to know you'd have come if I had."

For a long moment he held her gaze with his own, and there was a serious note in his voice when he spoke again.

"You couldn't ever doubt that I would, could you, Sally?" he said gently. "You *know* I'll come for you . . . anywhere, any time. But," he was smiling again, "who-ever we have to thank let's make the most of it. Tell me, how are they treating you here?"

CHAPTER TWELVE

THEY spent a happy afternoon together, and Sally was delighted to find that Mike was, as she had always known him, willing to allow their friendship to remain on whatever footing she chose. When the first moments were over he did not again refer to the question of why or how he had been called to Queen's Close, apparently taking it for granted that, since Sally was pleased to see him and he was obeying the summons of old Samuel himself, all must be well. They talked of the varied assignments he had been out upon since their last meeting and of one or two interesting forthcoming events to which he hoped she would be able to accompany him. Ivy brought them tea, and shortly after that Mike decided it was time he should be going.

"I don't know whose idea this was, Sally," he said on leaving, "but it was a good one. Mr. Bodman has told me to come whenever I like and says you're to telephone me or leave word at the office if you have any unexpected free time. I could almost think," he laughed teasingly, "the old boy was on my side . . . if I didn't know he never 'meddled', as he calls it, in the affairs of anyone but those of his own family."

When Mike had gone, Sally went slowly back to Francie's room. Already an idea had been forming in her mind, and she was anxious to know if her guess was the right one. The family rose almost in a body as she came in, and she knew from the way in which they were anxiously awaiting reassurance that they had not tired the patient, that she would have full co-operation from each and every one of them, a knowledge which lifted a certain amount of worry from her mind, for she had been a little afraid that in the confines of her own home Stella Bodman might prove difficult.

Francie had certainly had enough excitement for one day. She *was* tired, but very happy and far more contented than she had been all the time Sally had been with her. As she was settled for the evening, Francie gave a long, satisfied sigh.

"Ivy's promised a specially attractive light dinner for us," she said contentedly. "That means most of the things I like best. Grandfather insists we keep to hospital routine as much as possible, so that means lights out at ten. I suppose you'll be able to go and watch television, or have a game of cards or talk to the others in the lounge for a while afterwards," she went on a trifle wistfully. "I don't mind. In fact, I'm pleased; it may not be like being with your friends, but I think you'll like the family once you get to know them better. If only Martin had come to-night," she sighed again, "everything would have been perfect." She waited a moment, then, as Sally did not speak, spoke the words which had evidently been uppermost in her mind for the past few minutes. "I don't suppose he gave your friend any message for me, did he?" she asked.

Sally wrinkled her forehead, then her brow cleared. Of course, her guess had been right. Francie was the one responsible for Mike's being at the house that afternoon.

"No," she said slowly, "he didn't. Or if he did Mike didn't say anything, and it isn't like him to forget anything. By the way, Francie, it was your idea, wasn't it, to have Mike come here?"

"Yes." A faint colour crept into Francie's cheeks. "I thought it would be nice if you had one of your own friends here for a little while, all of us being strangers and everything so different. I thought it would make you . . . settle down better."

"And is that all?" Sally persisted relentlessly but with a faint smile. "Is that the only reason?"

"Not really." The colour deepened. "Don't be cross, Sally," she said pleadingly. "I don't know how much Mike means to you, but I do know he is a good friend of yours and that you go around with him, so I didn't think you would mind. And after all, he works with Martin, and they like each other. Martin says Mike is one of the best reporters the paper has ever had or is likely to have, and Mike said once—you told me so yourself—that Martin was wonderful to work with, so . . ."

"So you allowed your grandfather and your parents to think . . . I don't know quite what they *did* think," Sally said helplessly. "That Mike and I were on the point of being engaged or something, I suppose, when the truth is that we're just extremely good friends. I'm not cross," she added hastily as she saw Francie's obvious signs of distress. "It's just that I'm used to making my own arrangements, deciding when I want to see my friends, all that sort of thing. Mike and I are . . . well, we're good friends in a special sort of way. I—your grandfather told me I could invite my friends here while I was looking after you, and I expect I would have invited him here before very long, but to have him here, the first day and without my knowing he was coming, well, it was a sort of shock. Oh, it was a pleasant one," she amended hastily as she saw Francie's face, "but . . . well, Mike and I are at the stage where I don't want to give him any false encouragement."

"He's really in love with you, isn't he, Sally?" Francie sighed. "And you either don't want him or can't make up your mind for some reason or another. It's none of my business," she added truthfully, "but I'd like to see you both really happy, the way I'd like to be happy with Martin, but he won't let himself be happy. He'd rather have his pride, and pride's cold comfort," she ended wistfully. "Especially when it's the wrong sort of pride."

"I'm no authority." Sally spoke briskly on purpose. She did not want to become involved in a discussion on her own emotional life just then, she was still wondering what conclusion the Bodman family had drawn from Francie's request to have Mike come to visit her almost before she had settled into the house. "Pride has its uses," she went on, "and most of us would be poor sort of people without *some* share of it. And now"—she looked up as the door opened and Ivy came in, pushing the dumb waiter—"here's Ivy with our dinner, and I must admit I'm ready for mine. But"—she held up one finger warningly—"I don't want any more talk about either Mike or

Martin until we've finished eating. In fact, I think we've heard quite enough about either of them for today."

"Just tell me one thing," Francie begged as the door closed behind the obviously interested Ivy, "if Martin had said anything, if he *had* any message for me, Mike would have brought it, wouldn't he? He wouldn't forget?"

"Anything Martin asks Mike to do is done," Sally assured her, striving for a light note in view of the seriousness of Francie's expression. "It's part of his job. Don't forget, Martin is his immediate boss. Your grandfather is the sort of remote control, as it were. It's to Martin that Mike is answerable if he forgets anything, so he always remembers!"

"I'll think of something." Francie's determined tone shocked Sally. "I must. Martin can never love anyone else as I know he loves me, and as for me, there isn't anyone in the world to compare with him. If only there was some way to make him *jealous*," she said suddenly. "If he thought there was someone else . . but how am I to meet anyone else cooped up here in a worse position than I was in the beginning?" Suddenly she pushed her plate on one side, her expression changing from one of defiance to a sort of hopeless resignation. "It's no use, is it, Sally?" she said soberly. "If a miracle happened and someone came along right now, say someone to visit Grandfather or someone else in the family, and I pretended we'd fallen in love at first sight or something like that, I guess Martin would just write me a congratulatory note and wish me well, or maybe he wouldn't even bother to do that. Maybe he'd just shrug his shoulders, the way he does when things don't go just the way he wants them to and there doesn't appear to be anything he can do about it . . . and that would be that."

"You're getting morbid," Sally said briskly, smiling and helping Francie with the cup of coffee she had just poured. "I think it's time you were settled down for the night. You'll feel a whole lot better in the morning, I'm sure. Concentrate on getting well. Keep giving your messages to Mike—he'll be here often enough, and—who knows?—maybe in time Martin will come and see you, and in the meantime we'll both try and think of something."

"Will you, Sally? Promise?" Francie asked, and as Sally nodded she looked contented and almost happy once more. "I shall sleep better now," she confessed. "I'm sure, between us, you and Mike and me, we'll think of some way to show Martin he's wrong."

She turned her head on the pillow and Sally shaded the light. The bell which connected with the room she had been given next door was within easy reach, but somehow she did not think Francie would have much use for it until morning.

She went softly from the room some minutes later, but she only looked in at the lounge to say goodnight. She felt suddenly very tired, far more tired than if she had worked a full day at the General as usual.

'Must be emotional fatigue,' she told herself as she prepared for bed. 'Leaving my friends . . . coming here, being made almost one of the family . . . Mr. Bodman's giving me the watch . . . Mike being here . . . everything has been in sort of overtones today. I think I'm like Francie and a good night's rest is what's needed to put things in perspective for me, too.'

She was soon ready for bed, not too tired to appreciate the beauty of the room, the carefully thought-out little touches which made her feel more a guest than someone who had come to Queen's Close to work: the biscuits in the little barrel, the small spirit kettle and the tea-set for one beside the bed, the pile of new novels and magazines, to say nothing of the carefully arranged flowers in the room; all spoke of loving care and forethought.

'All this for a stranger,' Sally mused as she put out the light and slipped between the clean, fragant sheets on the most comfortable bed she had ever known in her life. 'What kindness, thought and love they must have given to Francie. If only they hadn't succeeded in almost smothering her with it all!'

She settled down and tried to get off to sleep, but sleep was elusive that night. She missed her usual chat with

Betty, and time and again her thoughts returned to the hospital as she wondered what everyone was doing there at that moment. After the hospital, because thoughts of Curtis Palmer were too disturbing, she made herself think of Mike, wishing sincerely that she could return the love there was no doubt he felt for her, but knowing in her secret heart that this was impossible.

At last she thought of Martin and Francie, each loving the other and held apart only by the barrier of Martin's pride which, while appreciating the care and thought that the Bodman money had given to his beloved, resented it because he could never hope to offer her the same himself, unless a miracle happened.

'It's all wrong,' she told herself, as she turned over yet again and tried to compose herself for sleep. 'I'm worrying because Curtis Palmer will never see me except as a nurse on the staff or as a friend of Mike's. Francie is worrying because Martin won't see anything except that the Bodmans have more money than he has, and Martin is worrying because he loves Francie and doesn't want to be unfair to her, to ask her something, knowing what the answer will be, in case she regrets it later. And Mike . . .' in the darkness she allowed herself a tender little smile for Mike, 'dear, *dear* Mike who loves me better than I deserve to be loved . . . and whom I like and, in one way, think the world of, but not in the way he wants. And Betty and Peter aren't settled . . . It's all so confusing. I think Curtis is the wisest one of us, putting his heart and soul into his work and leaving human relationships out of it all.'

She was still thinking of him and of his lovely, well-groomed mother whom he obviously adored, as she fell asleep at last, and in no time at all it seemed the alarm bell of her little travelling clock was ringing and it was time to get up.

Sally had just pushed back the sheet when there was a soft tap on her bedroom door and it opened to admit Ivy, carrying a small, daintily appointed tray.

"Mrs. Bodman thought you might like a cup of tea before you go in to Miss Francie, Nurse Sally," she said, drawing back the curtains. "Isn't it a lovely morning?" she rattled on. "This rate June'll be a glorious month, just like it's supposed to be."

"It certainly will." Sally accepted the tea gratefully, and the plate of attractive-looking biscuits which lay beside it. "You and Mrs. Bodman will spoil me, Ivy." She smiled. "I'm not used to this sort of thing."

"A little spoiling, as you call it, won't do you any harm, Nurse Sally, and that's a fact," Ivy returned. "When I was at school the teacher once asked me if I'd like to take up nursing. 'You have a gift for looking after others, Ivy,' was what she said. That's as maybe, was what I told her, but there's looking after folks *and* looking after 'em, if you get what I mean. I couldn't do the work *you* do, nor have I the patience with poorly folks you must have. I can clean and cook and serve, but I'd not be much good in a sickroom for any length of time. That's unless it was someone of my own folks who were ill, or someone like Miss Francie, who's as dear as my own folk to me. I just know I couldn't do it for strangers."

"We're all human, Ivy," Sally reminded her, smiling. "We don't have to think of patients as individuals. Just as people, people who are hurt, who are sick, and whom we can help back to health and strength again, whoever they may be."

"Well, takes all sorts to make a world, as my mum always says. Wouldn't do for us all to be nurses, now, would it? Or all of us to be gardeners and what-have-you like my Ned. He'd be in a sorry state if he happened an accident, say mowing the lawns or with the tractor when he's down in the fields, if there weren't any doctors or folks who knew what to do."

"As your mum said," Sally smiled, "it takes all sorts to make a world, gardeners as well as doctors—what's the matter, Ivy?" she added, as the girl suddenly clapped a hand to her mouth, her face full of consternation.

"If that isn't like me," she cried. "Mrs. Bodman always says I'd forget my head if it wasn't fixed on to my neck! They telephoned from the hospital this morning and said they were sending a mobile . . . physical something it sounded like, out here for ten o'clock."

"Mobile physiotherapy unit," Sally said quickly. "Good. That means one step nearer to Miss Francie's walking again. I must get a move on, Ivy, and have everything ready for them."

"I'll run your bath, Nurse," Ivy offered. "I can do it for you regularly if you like."

Sally did not know whether to be amused or flattered by Ivy's little extra attentions, but it was plain the girl shared the family feeling of gratitude to the nurse who had saved Miss Francie's life.

With Ivy's help she was soon attending to her patient, and Francie, new colour in her cheeks, new hope in her heart for some reason which Sally could not even guess, was ready and waiting by the time the unit arrived. It had been decided before they left the General that her next visit to therapy would see Francie attempting to walk, using crutches. She made the attempt that morning, and, accustomed as she was to seeing patients make their first fumbling steps back along the road to recovery, Sally found an unaccustomed ache in her heart as she watched the small, slim figure bravely trying to master the new technique of this form of locomotion. She was so absorbed in Francie's efforts and the brave way in which she was making herself follow instructions that she did not notice the low, silver-grey car which halted before the house and below the terrace on which Francie was making her first halting steps.

"Doing quite well, isn't she, Nurse?" Sally started, and the tell-tale colour flew into her cheeks at the sound of Curtis Palmer's voice. With an effort she pulled herself together.

"At this rate she will soon be able to manage without the crutches, sir," she said, in her best professional manner. "She's determined to walk again, and that's more than half the battle."

"It is, indeed." Curtis looked at her, fresh and neat in her crisp white and blue uniform, a few tendrils of her softly waving chestnut brown hair escaping from her cap and blowing gently against her cheek in the soft wind from the garden.

"Must we be so formal . . . here?" he asked softly. "Mrs. Bodman particularly asked us not to be. She doesn't want the hospital atmosphere around the home. I can manage to drop it for a time if you can . . . Sally."

"Just as you say," Sally said primly, her heart racing as she told herself not to be foolish enough as to read anything other than the exact words he uttered into his remarks. "It will seem strange, though."

"So do most things, until they become a habit," Curtis said enigmatically, then a moment later he was approaching Francie and had taken her by the hands, helping her to the chair ready and waiting for her.

"You've done splendidly," he praised the girl. "Keep up your exercises, and your rest . . . in that order. Do as Nurse Sally tells you, and before June is out I think you'll be well able to manage with, perhaps, the help of a stick. And it will only be a matter of time before that can be discarded as well."

"I can't believe it," Francie said, her eyes shining as she looked up at him, so that, abruptly, Sally had a sudden memory of Matron's warning and she wondered whether the girl knew how lovely she looked, how attractive, sitting looking up at Curtis with that melting appeal in her violet-blue eyes.

'She said she wanted to try and make Martin jealous,' Sally remembered the conversation of the previous evening. 'I wonder . . . she couldn't, not with Curtis. If he were ever serious about a girl it would break his heart, embitter him for ever, if she were not true to him.'

"And it's all due to you and Sally and . . . oh, I don't know, everybody's been so kind and so helpful. I feel I can't do enough to repay you all."

"Just get strong again," Curtis said gently. "That's all the reward we ask."

"There are other things," Francie pouted. "Grand-father knows what's best . . . I shall have a talk with him . . . but there must be things I haven't thought of." She wrinkled her forehead, thinking, and Sally had a sudden dread that somehow she was about to drag Mike into the conversation. Before she had an opportunity to say anything, however, Ivy appeared beside them.

"You're wanted on the telephone, Nurse," she said. "I think it's a friend of yours . . . another nurse. No need to hurry . . ." But Sally had seen Curtis's eyebrows go up at the mention of the word 'friend', and with all her heart she longed to run straight back from the telephone and inform him her caller was only Betty, wanting to know when Sally had some free time.

She chatted to Betty for a while, and when she went back to the terrace Curtis was ready to leave. He looked at Sally before he turned to descend the steps from the terrace, and for no real reason she had the feeling he was trying to give her a message, but what it could be she had no idea. Together she and Francie watched him drive away, and, scarcely listening to what the other girl was saying, Sally moved like an automaton, knowing now what she had so far refused to face as the truth, that she loved Curtis Palmer with her whole heart, mind and body, and that so long as she lived no other man would ever mean so much to her as he did and always would.

CHAPTER THIRTEEN

THE knowledge that she really loved Curtis Palmer and was not going through a stage so familiar to a lot of the nurses at the General, of simply having a 'crush' on him which would, in due course, burn itself out, was something of a shock so far as Sally was concerned. Had she not been aware of how completely Francie relied upon her, trusted her in every possible way, she would have been tempted to go and see Matron and ask to be taken off the case.

'I'd see him at the hospital,' she told herself, 'but it's different there, somehow. The entire atmosphere is different. It's so like a family gathering every time he comes to Queen's Close. It seems such an . . . intimate atmosphere.'

Sally did her best to instil something of the discipline of the wards into every visit Curtis made to the house, and he called every day, but all in vain. Francie had made a friend of him, Stella and Robert knew him well, and of course old Samuel thought the world of him and was never tired of saying how lucky the General was to have him there. Sally was made to feel one of them, and it was impossible to make any impression on any of them. In fact, at times she felt they were all laughing at her attempts to put matters on to a more formal footing, laughing with kindly laughter, but laughing just the same.

"It doesn't seem the right thing to do," she protested on one occasion when, timing its arrival for the moment when Francie's exercises were over for the day, Stella had Ivy bring out a tea of early strawberries and cream for them all. "I mean . . ."

"What Sally means," Curtis glanced at her briefly across the low table as he spooned sugar over his strawberries, "is that back at the General she would be having tea in the nurses' home along with all the other nurses, and I would be having mine in the consultants' dining-room; a grim business at times, I do assure you." His eyes were twinkling and there was a little smile playing around the corners of his mouth as he spoke. "It may not seem the right thing to do, Nurse," he went on, addressing her directly, "but I'm sure it's a *good* thing to do. A change is as good as a rest, or so they say, in certain conditions, and I'm certain this change has been almost as good for you as for our patient. You certainly look much less under strain than when you came here and, if I may say so, prettier than ever."

"Then it must be all right, if you say so," Sally murmured, and only just managed to bite back the word 'sir', since he had forbidden her to address him so formally while they were at Queen's Close.

She ate her tea in almost complete silence, listening as the other chattered and speaking only when directly

addressed, but she was aware of Curtis watching her
closely, and the knowledge did nothing to still the tumult
of her heart. She excused herself from the table as soon
as she decently could and went into her own room,
intending to stay there until Curtis had left, but, some
time later, she was summoned by the little bell which had
been connected so that Francie could call her if necessary
at any hour of the day or night.

Sally went back on to the terrace to find Curtis ready
to leave. He looked down at her with a smile as she came
quietly to join them.

"I wanted to see you before I left, Sally," he said
lightly. "Matron thinks you can carry on from here, that
the therapy people need not come out again unless you
want them to. Do you think you can manage? Francie is
doing remarkably well. It's mid-June now; by the end of
the month she should be able to walk with just one stick
. . . then a week or two more and she should be able to
manage without any extra support at all, and your work
here will be ended. You do agree with me, don't you?" he
shot at her abruptly.

"I do," Sally nodded, quite content to keep the conversation on this level, but wishing that being so close to
Curtis did not have this strange effect upon her pulse-
rate. "Francie has tried very hard, and she doesn't give in
easily."

"Not in anything," Francie put in from her couch
where she had been avidly listening. "Remember, Sally,
I've told you one or two plans I don't intend to let
go . . .?"

"I hope they're good ones, then," Curtis said, still
smiling. "Walk to the car with me, Sally. I just want to
have a word with you about the new tablets. They should
put the finishing touch to rebuilding Francie's vitality,
but any excess might not be wise . . ."

They walked from the terrace down the drive together,
Curtis still talking about the new tablets and their effect
upon one or two other patients who had been subjected
to fierce shock, and all the time Sally felt she was making
the wrong answers, not really thinking what she said,

but wondering why he wanted to walk with her to his car to say what could obviously have been said just as well on the terrace.

He paused at the door of his car and looked down at her, his glance speculative.

"You're a good nurse, Sally," he said, and the unexpected compliment brought the ready colour to her cheeks. "Tell me," he went on, "are you also a dedicated one?"

"I don't know what you mean." Sally wrinkled her forehead as she tried to decide exactly what Curtis *could* mean by such a remark. "If you mean do I put my patient's welfare before my own . . . yes. If you mean do I give myself up wholly and solely to nursing, think of it, dream of it, make it my be-all and end-all . . . then I'm afraid the answer is no."

"I did mean something like that," Curtis confessed, "but I also meant . . . have you ever thought of yourself as doing anything else, having a home and a life of your own, as an instance?"

"Some day." Sally knew her colour had risen again, but that was something she could not control. "Every girl has that kind of dream, I think," she said softly. Curtis nodded, looked as though he were about to say something else and then saw Samuel descending the terrace steps to join them and changed his mind.

"See you tomorrow," he said briefly, giving her a small salute before getting into his car and then driving away before Sam could catch up and keep them talking.

"Busy chap," the old gentleman observed, coming to a halt beside Sally. "Glad he's with us at the General. Must get him to tell me just how much money will be needed for all this new equipment he says he could do with. We need, says he, another heart and lung machine, another theatre . . . oh, I don't know what, but I'll be glad to help. Rather do it this way than be endowing something as a memorial to my little Francie."

Abruptly Sally remembered that the hospital had already a women's surgical ward which had been endowed by Samuel in memory of his wife, many years previously, and that there were cots in the children's ward which he had also endowed, grateful for what had been done for the children of Barcaster. Francie might bemoan the fact that the Bodman money stood between herself and Martin, but it had certainly done a great deal of good for a number of people over the years.

She had more evidence of the generosity of the Bodmans as the days went by. Ned, Ivy's fiancé, had started work as a gardener's boy on the estate when he first left school. Thanks to Robert he had been given his chance at the Agricultural College, and now he was in charge of all the men working on the extensive estate and nearby Home Farm.

"He's saved me another fortune, has that young man," old Sam confided in Sally one day when Ned had called at the house with some special produce with which he had been experimenting. "There's nothing like the land for swallowing good money, unless you have a head on you to know what you're doing, and he certainly does. I shall do my best for him and for Ivy ... she's a good girl."

Do his best the old man certainly did, and when Ivy proudly showed Sally round the little house on the estate which was being got ready for them, Sally had to admit that nothing had been left out which would add to the comfort and easy running of a modern home.

"There's even a new-fangled what-do-you-call-it for waste, rubbish and the like," Ivy pointed out the waste-disposal unit with justifiable pride. "And central heating. When I remember how my mum managed, heating her water in an old copper thing, carrying it from the pump until we got the taps and that in, I can't believe how lucky I am. There's certainly nothing better than working for the Bodmans ... if you do what's right, that is. But I've heard tell it's not such a bed of roses if you try anything you shouldn't. That's more than me and my Ned'll ever do. We know when we're being looked after, and it don't hurt to give good service in return."

Sally too knew when she was 'being well looked after'. She had never been so cosseted or so comfortable in her life, not even at home. She was not lonely either, for

Stella Bodman had been to the hospital and had a discreet chat with Matron, and after that, Betty and most of the nurses who were friends of Sally were able to pop up to Queen's Close and be made welcome whenever they had a free time off duty.

"I should try to spin this out at least through the summer," Betty had said on one occasion as they relaxed after a session in the swimming-pool which had been created especially for Francie, but which she had seldom used until now, when Sally had pointed out to her just how much such exercise would help her regain strength in the muscles of her back and legs. "And just think, if it went on and on . . . I bet Christmas is marvellous here in this lovely old house."

"It's marvellous at the General, too," Sally smiled at her friend, "and the way Francie's improving I don't think I shall need to be here much longer, anyway."

"You don't sound too depressed by the thought of returning to normal duty," Betty teased. "You'll still see Curtis."

"I know." Sally's lips tightened a little. The urge to confide in her friend was there, but what was there to tell? Only that he came daily, that he always made it in his way to have a little chat with her, either before he had attended Francie or before he left, and that both he and Sally knew that his visits were no longer really necessary and that there must, in that case, be some other reason for his daily call.

Sally would not allow herself to dream that she might be the reason. He had said nothing, done nothing, to justify such a thought, yet he made no move to see Francie alone either, and apart from the fact that the girl obviously thought him a wonderful man, she never spoke of him in any intimate way or indicated that she, as so many before her had done, had fallen for his undoubted charm.

'But she doesn't talk about Martin either, now,' Sally reflected, scarcely listening to Betty's chatter, immersed as she was in her own thoughts. 'She never mentions him . . . I wonder if all that has fizzled out?'

"It would be nice if you—changed your mind about Mike, and we could all live somewhere near each other," Betty was saying, and with a start Sally realised that for some time past she had not been listening to her friend.

"What did you say?" she asked apologetically. "I'm sorry, I must have been day-dreaming."

"I said Pete and I are hovering on the brink of an engagement, and you don't even listen," Betty said reproachfully. "I told you he intends setting up in partnership with his father in due course. Well, Dr. Brady has a practice in Litherthorpe, and that's only about ten miles from Barcaster. I said," she repeated with deliberation, "that it was a pity you couldn't change your mind about Mike. There's some land for sale between Barcaster and Litherthorpe, just enough for two smart houses and an extension surgery. I said," she emphasised, "it would be nice if we could all live somewhere near to each other . . ."

Sally sat upright on the grass, her gaze fixed on Francie, who had been practising walking, using her one stick now as little as possible and evidently about to attempt the descent from the terrace.

"I shouldn't count on that, if I were you," she said slowly, knowing that she had made up her mind only at that instant, but knowing too that she would not change it. "Mike is coming up here tonight. Mr. Bodman asked him to bring some papers . . . I don't know whether he really wants them or whether he considers he's helping in some way, but there we are." She paused a moment, then added, dramatically but quietly: "I shall tell Mike tonight that my mind is made up. He keeps proposing, I keep refusing. That isn't fair, because he always goes on hoping that I'll change my mind. Tonight I must tell him that I never will . . . change it, I mean. That it's time he found some other girl, asked for a change, went on to one of the other Bodman papers in some other town. It isn't fair to ruin his life in this way. Some day he'll find someone else who'll appreciate him for the wonderful person he is, and will return his love as he deserves to have it returned."

"Sally!" Betty, too, sat upright, staring at her friend as though she could not believe her ears. "Does that mean you've . . . found someone else?" she demanded.

"Not exactly." Sally's fingers plucked nervously at the closely cut grass, and she stared down at them unseeingly, satisfied that Francie was safely down the steps and walking carefully along the garden path. "I think, maybe, I'll never marry," she said slowly and uncertainly, an abrupt vista of lonely years ahead opening up before her. "I'll just go on and on . . . Ward Sister . . . learning all I can . . . maybe one day an Assistant Matron and then maybe a Matron . . ."

"You can't!" Betty spoke impulsively. "Oh"—she gesticulated wildly, aware of Sally's startled glance—"I don't mean you're not good enough or keen enough. You've done miles better than I have, all those extra courses and your maternity and everything . . . but somehow it just isn't *you*, Sally. You're meant for a cosy home, a man to love and a man who loves you. For a family of your own, who'll grow up around you and be there when you're old . . . not living out your days alone and lonely, giving your life to the service of countless thousands who won't even remember you when once they're well."

"To help them get well would be a wonderful thing," Sally returned slowly. "We can't all leave running the world and the care of those who need us to 'the others', there just aren't enough folks willing and able to go round to do all there is to do. Besides," she ended defiantly, "isn't it better to let Mike go . . . tell him to definitely look for someone else . . . than to keep him hanging on when I know now there'll never be the answer he's waiting for . . . from me?"

"I suppose it is," Betty agreed slowly, "but don't tell him today. I'll have to be going in a few minutes, and I want to ask you something first. Will you and Mike come and have a drink with us at the Blue Grill Room to-morrow? Say, round about six, if they'll let you come then. We're going to buy an engagement ring, and I'd like you and Mike to be the first to see it."

"I'll tell him tomorrow, then," Sally agreed. "One day

can't make all that much difference, and anyway, your getting engaged will be sure to start him off on another proposal, bless his heart, and then I'll tell him the truth . . . that I've made up my mind and he's not to go on wasting any more of his life on me. It's been fun, going around with him all this time, and we've had some great times together, but it's unfair to Mike, and I'm going to put an end to it before my resolution weakens."

"If it's because of the person I see has just arrived," Betty remarked, scrambling to her feet and beginning to gather up her personal things from the grass, "then I think you're a fool. Look at him. If he thinks his getting the new equipment depends on his being the son-in-law, then bang goes any romantic dream you might have been cherishing. By the way, what's happened about that Martin chap, the editor? Have you heard anything of him, about his work . . . anything?"

"Nothing much," Sally answered, her gaze fixed on the tall figure of Curtis, who was bending over Francie, talking to her. "Old Mr. Bodman said he had finished the book he was working on and he'd sent it to an agent Mr. Bodman recommended and that the agent thought it extremely good. That was all. I don't know whether he's found a publisher yet or whatever these folks do when they've written a book, but Mr. Bodman says he's a young man with a wonderful future."

"Yes, maybe," Betty's tone was sceptical, "but by the time he's achieved what he's after it will be too late. Francie will have found someone else."

"I don't think so." Sally knew she was saying this to try and make herself believe it was so, but when she looked at her patient, so lovely and so appealing, looking up at the handsome young surgeon, it was hard to believe they were not made for each other.

"I must be off," Betty decided. "Mr. Bodman said Ned was going down into Barcaster and would give me a lift back, and I can see the big estate car at the foot of the steps. Thanks for a lovely afternoon, Sally." She smiled briefly. "I shall thank Mrs. Bodman and the family, of course. I know it's their house and they are the hosts, but

I wouldn't have been here if you hadn't saved Francie *and* nursed her so well afterwards, so it's you I'm thanking first and right now."

"I love having you," Sally said truthfully. "I still miss our little nightly exchange of gossip . . . all the luxury in the world doesn't make up for friends."

"That's what Francie found out, isn't it?" Betty. was ready to go now. "But she seems to be making up for it. Anyhow, let Mike off until after our little celebration, there's a dear. It would spoil everything if you told him tonight and then he refused to come."

"All right," Sally promised, and made herself wave a cheerful goodbye as Betty was soon driven away sitting beside the stolid Ned on the front seat of the large shooting brake which he ran to town for the Bodman family's convenience.

She had thought Curtis was about to leave without a word with her, and with a sharp pang she realised that if he did this would mark the beginning of a new pattern, for so far on every visit he had contrived to have at least a few words, not always about Francie. She had thought he was walking towards his car, but he left the path and walked across the grass to the pool, smiling as he greeted her.

"Francie tells me you've taught her to swim," he remarked, and he drew closer. "I'm delighted. I think every child should be taught when they're very young. Save an awful lot of lives if they were. Who taught you, Sally?"

"My brother," Sally told him, remembering. "At least, we went together for swimming lessons and he was a natural swimmer. I just couldn't let him beat me, so I learned quickly too."

"Good for you," Curtis observed. "I like that. You don't let many things 'beat you', do you, Sally? It's a good thing to have that determination, *and* the heart and spirit to try in the first place, not to be afraid of defeat. Still"—he gave a small smile and a shrug—"we all have our little failings. I"—he gave another slight smile—"am afraid—always—of emotional defeat. An operation, however tricky, is a challenge. A . . . request . . . something where there is a chance of a refusal . . . that's a different matter. Sally"—he was suddenly very serious and there was no smile now on his face—"if you were in my shoes I wonder what you would do? I want to find out something, to ask someone a question, and I desperately want the answer to go the way I want it, but I'm so afraid that it may not turn out like that. That there may be . . . obstacles in the way, for I'm not at all sure. What would you do?"

"Is there only this one person who could answer your question, then?" Sally asked, wondering whether he was thinking of Francie and whether or not he could ask her to marry him, or of Sam, Robert, Stella and the Bodman money and wondering if that might be the 'obstacle' in the way.

"Only the one person, Sally," Curtis told her gravely. "And I'm . . . afraid of what the answer might be."

"I wouldn't be afraid." Sally summoned all her courage to the fore. If he had to have Francie, then she would help him if she could. But she must talk with Francie first and make quite certain that the dream of Martin was gone for ever and that Curtis was not to be used as a substitute. "I'd . . . ask my question. If you don't ask it, then you'll never know the answer, will you? And it might well be the answer you want. You can't tell if you don't ask."

"True, true." Curtis nodded his head in agreement. "I think you're right. I'll do that." He lifted his head as though indeed at the moment he had accepted a challenge. "Before the week is out," he added gravely, as though he were making a solemn promise to himself. Abruptly his mood changed and he smiled at her with the slow, disturbingly sweet smile which did such strange things to her heart.

"You'll be here tomorrow, Sally?" he stated rather than asked, but Sally shook her head.

"Not unless you're here in the morning," she told him. "I have the afternoon and evening free tomorrow. I'm going into Barcaster. I have a date with Betty and some others."

"Then . . . until the day after." Curtis gave her his customary brief salute, and as he went she wanted to call after him that she hoped when he asked his question the answer would be the right one, but the words just would not come. She raised her hand as he drove away, then went slowly back to the house, determined, even if it made Francie angry, to make sure that Curtis was not being used as a balm to Francie's hurt Bodman pride, and that if it were Francie's hand in marriage he was seeking, then that Francie now had experienced a change of heart and would not be marrying one man with the ghost of another between them.

CHAPTER FOURTEEN

WHEN, much later, Sally came to look back at that evening she realised it was one of the most important evenings of her life. She had taken Francie to her own room, and the girl was excited because her mother had suggested it was time she moved back to her own rooms upstairs.

"You can have the room next door," Francie chattered on. "It used to be my nannie's when I was a little girl, and there's a communicating bathroom. You can use the other one on the other side of the corridor if you like, of course. I'll speak to Mummy . . ."

"I really think," Sally said as she helped Francie change her dress, "that it will soon be time I was going back to the hospital. You're strong enough to look after yourself, you have Ivy and the others to help you, and if you keep up your exercises and your swimming you'll be as fit as ever you were before the summer's ended."

"But I won't have *you*, Sally," Francie protested. "You're like all the rest . . . here for a time, then gone, for ever. Martin"—her voice choked suddenly—"was like that. When we first went around together he was often here. When he—when we—fell in love, he came less and

E

less often, and then he didn't come at all. Said he had his book to write, made that his excuse, and then he told me the truth . . . this dreadful money came right between us . . . and when you get back to your friends and you're going to the Copper Bowl and all the other places together, you'll forget all about me . . . you'll never come again, either."

"I will, of course I will," Sally promised sincerely. "I love it here, and you've all been so good to me. But there are other people who are sick, Francie. There is a shortage of nurses. My 'compassionate leave' has already been extended twice, and that's more than would have been done for me, unless in very exceptional circumstances, if I'd been nursing someone at my own home . . ."

"I know." Francie sat down on the edge of her bed looking like a disappointed child. "You don't have to tell me, it's because of all the family have done for the General in the past and the fact that Grandfather is Chairman of the Committee . . . the old, old story. Just as Martin said, it's too big to beat, and you can't join and keep your pride."

"Then Martin, on that occasion at any rate, talked a great deal of nonsense," Sally said sharply. Then she added, aware that the shock of her question might startle Francie into saying more than she would have done had she approached the matter cautiously. "What about Martin these days? I heard what your grandfather said about his book and his agent, but . . ."

"That's all I know, too," Francie said, lifting her head defiantly. "Wait just a little longer, Sally, and you'll see. I've learned a great deal from you, and I intend to put some of it into practice. You aren't afraid . . . or if you are you don't show it. And I'm not going to be afraid either. As soon as I feel I can drive my car again I'm going to see Martin. I'm going to make him change his mind. I don't know how, but I'm going to. I shall tell him lies, tell him I've fallen for my doctor, tell him *anything* to make him jealous enough to admit he cares and that it would break his heart if I had."

"But," Sally nerved herself and made the words come

out although every one seemed like a knife in her heart, "is that fair to Mr. Palmer?" she asked gently. "Is that a right thing to do? To let him think you may be willing to marry him, and all the time you're using him to try and force Martin's hand..."

"Fair?" To Sally's utter amazement Francie burst into laughter. "It's Mr. Palmer's idea," she said gaily. "I ... I don't know what made me tell him about Martin, but we were talking about writers and what kind of people they must be, and I said I knew one, and before I knew what was happening I'd told him everything, all about what I was doing on the parapet of the bridge, all about Martin being proud and wanting to earn enough money for us and about my saying I'd be satisfied whatever he earned and he saying I didn't know what it would be like. You needn't worry about Mr. Palmer," she ended before she paused for breath, "he only sees me as an 'interesting case'. He told me so," she ended with a sudden impish smile which told Sally she was indeed speaking the truth.

"Then what do you plan to do?" Sally asked when she felt she could trust her voice not to give away any of the emotion that was pulling at her heart. "Have you made any plans?"

"Not yet, but I will," Francie said lightly. "Not to worry, Sally. I'll have it all worked out, and if Martin needs shock tactics to get him moving, then shock tactics it must be. Now, you go down to dinner. You can wait at the foot of the stairs ... catch me if I fall down them ... but I'm determined to make the effort entirely on my own tonight."

Obediently Sally went downstairs and was joined by old Sam as she waited for Francie to descend.

"She's looking much better," the old man remarked, eyeing Sally with the twinkle she loved. "It's a great deal to do with the friendship which has grown between you two, Sally," he went on unexpectedly. "I'm very grateful. We all are. If only I knew what made her go up on to that parapet in the first place..."

"I expect she'll tell you ... one day," Sally said a little absent-mindedly, since she was concentrating on watching

Francie negotiate the stairs. "She said she wanted to talk to you."

"She knows I'll always listen, and that I won't kick up a fuss, whatever she has to tell me."

"I know." Sally went to help Francie round the newel post with the carved top, a difficult move until she could walk and stand with greater ease. "I'm sure you'll be able to help," she added, giving him a reassuring smile before she praised Francie for her efforts and they all walked together into the long dining-room.

After dinner Sally was amused to see how old Sam manoeuvred them all until he had Sally playing cards with Robert and Stella and Mike, who had called and brought the required papers and found himself hustled into the game, while he asked Francie to walk round his new conservatory with him. They were gone a long time, and Sally knew without being told the old man had taken the opportunity of finding out for himself just what was wrong, what it was that had made his beloved grand-daughter seek such dangerous solitude.

She went to the door to see Mike off, wishing she had not given her promise to Betty, feeling suddenly that it was most unfair to have Mike adoring her, wanting her to marry him, when she knew now that however much she liked him she could never think of him as anything but a very dear friend, and she felt absurdly grateful that tonight he made no romantic moves which might have upset her and caused her to break her promise. Instead he gave her an almost brotherly kiss and a slight hug, saying as he climbed into his little car, "See you at the Blue Grill Room tomorrow? Betty rang me up and said she and Pete had a surprise all planned. She said you'd promised to be there. We might do a flick. There's a thriller on at the Ritz which Tom Trent says is good. He's doing the reviews of the shows this week."

"We'll see, tomorrow," Sally answered. "If it's a fine evening I'd thought of the park."

"And a boat, and the lake ... the lot, I know!" Mike grinned good humouredly. "O.K." He switched on the engine. "I daresay you're right. If this weather is going to continue it seems a shame to be sitting indoors. See you tomorrow, then." And a moment later he was off down the drive.

Sally went indoors and said her goodnights, surprised to learn that Francie had already gone up to bed. When she said goodnight to Sam there was an extra twinkle in the blue eyes as his gaze met her own, but she didn't learn anything from him. He merely smiled, the corners of his mouth tilting in a mischievous way, as though he were well satisfied.

'If it all weren't so impossible ... breaking through the barrier of a man's pride, I mean,' Sally told herself as she mounted the beautiful staircase on her way to bed, 'I'd say he's found the solution, but how?'

There was no one she could ask. She could only wait and see whether or not Francie would confide in her. The other girl was almost ready for bed when Sally entered with her tablets and hot milk. She, too, looked as though she were well pleased with life, but all she said was: "I think it's all going to work out, Sally. If it doesn't, if Martin doesn't react the way I hope—and expect—he will, then I've lost him for ever, and landed myself in the soup as well." She smiled up at the nurse, sudden fear showing in the violet-blue eyes. "Wish me luck," she begged. "I'm sure it will have some effect, having your good wishes, I mean."

"You always have those," Sally assured her sincerely, "but won't you tell me what it is you've planned?"

"Not just yet," Francie said firmly. "The fewer people who know about this the better, but you needn't worry. Grandfather is helping me, and *he* thinks it will be all right. He knows Martin perhaps even better than I do."

"Well," Sally stifled a yawn, "whatever it is I hope for your sake it turns out well," she said, rinsing out the glass and making sure Francie was comfortably settled. "See you in the morning, and," she paused by the door, "you're doing splendidly," she said encouragingly. "As I said before, you soon won't need me at all."

"I shall always need you, Sally," Francie said in a suddenly serious tone. "I need your friendship, your ... I don't know how to put it, but it's something about you . . . your honesty, your faith and your kindness which is wonderful. You won't forget your promise to visit me when . . . after you go back to the hospital, will you?" she asked, her voice rising.

"Never." Sally shook her head. "I shall come and see you as often as you'd like me to," she said quietly. "You'll probably get tired of my company in the end. I shall remind you too much of what happened."

"I shall never get tired of your company, Sally." Francie snuggled down and smiled up at her. "I'm too grateful for what you did—what you're still doing—for me. I'm going to help myself as much as I can in the morning, then you can have a lovely long, free afternoon. Betty said she was planning some sort of celebration and she wanted you to share. I mustn't be selfish. She must miss you too."

"There are hundreds of other nurses at the General," Sally said lightly, but knowing that her friendship with Betty *was* something special and glad that Francie had shown no jealousy about it. "We'll wait and see what tomorrow brings," she ended as she went out of the room. "Ring if you need me. Goodnight."

There were no calls from Francie's room that night; there had not been any for many nights past. The nightmares had apparently ended as she gained in strength and the shock had subsided, and she no longer needed the heavy sedatives, but Sally found sleep a long time in coming to her, although she was tired. She could not help thinking about Curtis, wondering what he had meant by his remarks as he left. From him, her thoughts sped to Betty and her Pete. Pete, Betty said, had settled down a great deal lately and was anxious only for the day to come when he could put up his plate beside that of his father. Sally was glad for Betty's sake. There was no doubt about her love for the handsome young doctor, and surely, Sally told herself, once an engaged man with a home, a practice and a settled sort of life in view, he would forget all the wild parties, all the mad practical jokes, all the flirtations which had made up his life so far? She could only pray it would be so, for Betty's sake, and from the contemplation of her two friends her thoughts turned to Mike once more and what words she could possibly use to tell him she had decided their friendship must terminate.

'It isn't fair to him to go on as we are,' she told herself over and over again, and refused to admit the thought that, as well as it being a handicap to Mike in the search for the right girl, people, the Bodmans, as an instance, might also begin to think of her as Mike's exclusive property, and that, she told herself firmly, would never do.

For the first time since she had been at Queen's Close she failed to hear her alarm clock ring, and was quite startled when Ivy brought in her tea. She had a headache, which was most unusual for Sally, and even the swallowing of two little white tablets kept for just such an occasion failed to take effect for some time. Francie, to Sally's delight, had been as good as her word and was dressed and ready to go down for breakfast when Sally went in to her.

"I've got my swimming things on underneath," she confessed as they descended the stairs together. "Mr. Palmer says the swimming is a very important part of the exercises and I can walk round without you now if I keep to the paths and the terrace, but I don't think I'd venture into the pool alone . . . not yet."

"The sun is quite strong this morning," Sally observed. "When you've had a little rest we'll go down to the pool. I must confess I shall feel better if you've got that out of the way for the day."

The swimming exercise passed off very well. They had an early lunch, and when Sally had seen Francie settled in the swinging hammock she was free to leave.

"I'm going down to the town later, Nurse," Ned told her as she encountered him passing through the hall. "It'll be about fiveish. Shall I be able to give you a lift?"

"No, thanks all the same." Sally smiled at him, liking this rosy-cheeked, placid-eyed fiancé of Ivy's. "I'm not meeting my friends until six," she confided, "but I thought I'd like to do a bit of shopping, and the shops mostly close around five, so I'll get off now. I can get the bus at the gates, or not far away, anyhow."

She hurried to get ready, not stopping to change, knowing the bus, unlike Ned, would not wait if she were a few minutes late. Ned was in the hall as she descended the stairs and smiled at her, his eyes evidently appreciating the trim picture she presented.

"I'm going down to the tomato bed," he said. "I can run you down the drive. That's a fair step on a hot day."

Gratefully Sally climbed into the seat beside him and accepted a lift to the bus stop just outside the estate, then she settled to wait for the bus, waving a cheerful goodbye to Ned, who went off about the family business.

The bus was a few minutes late, but there were scarcely any passengers aboard. Sally climbed the stairs to her favourite seat, in the front on the top deck. There was no one else at all upstairs, and after a few moments she took out her cigarettes and lit up, relaxing and trying to stop worrying as to how best she could tell Mike that what she intended to do was as much for his benefit as her own.

He would be sure to ask if there was anyone else, and how could she, truthfully, say there was? In her heart there was . . . someone. Curtis Palmer, but did he know that she existed, except as a nurse who had been attending what he had classed as 'an interesting case'. A little smile played round the corners of her mouth as she recalled Francie telling her that was how Curtis thought of the richest girl in Barcaster. And yet . . . all the Bodman money could help someone like Curtis, someone with fingers which held the gift of healing.

'But he's happy where he is,' Sally told herself. 'I'm sure of that, and he couldn't be doing more important or more useful work, no matter where he went or what he did . . .'

She thought of Betty, as the bus approached the suburbs and trim houses with well-tended gardens came into view. Betty set a great deal of store by the house and the garden attached, she knew, but, she stifled a sigh, what would Betty say if Sally told her she would willingly live in a tent or a wooden hut, in the Arctic or in the jungle, if only Curtis told her he wanted her, needed her, *loved* her and wanted her with him?

'I mustn't think about him,' she chided herself firmly as the traffic thickened a few miles outside the sprawling old town. 'I must remember that he sees me as . . . a nurse. That he's been friendly because we've both been working at the Bodmans', and that as soon as I get back to the General everything will be on its old, formal footing again. It has to be. One can't have that kind of emotion—imagination—running wild in a hospital. I shall just have to get used to it, or leave and find somewhere else.'

She gazed idly through the window, no longer contented by her thoughts, but disturbed and uneasy, knowing that Mike would not willingly give up their friendship and knowing how lonely she was going to be with Betty and Pete absorbed in each other and no Mike to whisk her off on one or another of his varied assignments.

'I shall have to make another special friend,' she told herself firmly, 'or go around with the crowd,' but she knew she would do neither of those things . . . not yet.

A number of children were playing on the grass verges of the road, and suddenly Sally remembered it was half-term. There would probably be lots of them in the shops, accompanying their mothers, buying clothes for the forthcoming holidays, or alone, mooning round the counters, exasperating the assistants.

'Ah, well,' Sally smiled to herself as she remembered, 'I used to do exactly the same thing, especially round the record counters and places like that.'

The small blue mini was coming down the straight road from Barcaster when it caught her eye. It was not speeding, as so many of these tiny cars did, but coming at a steady, well-ordered speed and was approaching the bus at a steady rate when a child, playing on the grass verge, sent its ball speeding into the middle of the road. Automatically a warning sprang to Sally's lips, just as the bus driver swung his vehicle to the right in an effort to avoid the child, the mini swerving to the left as the bus must have appeared to loom up over its driver.

Sally had the sense to grab at the rail in front of the window as the brakes were applied, squealing in protest. Then there was a sickening impact as the bus caught the mini, and after that everything seemed to be strangely silent.

CHAPTER FIFTEEN

DESPITE the fact that she had caught hold of the rail in front of the window, the sudden braking of the bus had jerked Sally violently, and it was a moment or so before she had collected her startled wits. As soon as she realised she was not hurt but that the strange silence boded something awful, she swung out of her seat and hurried down the stairs to the conductor, standing on the roadway staring into the left-hand side of the road. Sally stared too, her eyes widening, for it was only too obvious what had happened. In spite of the efforts of the driver of the bus to avoid an accident, his heavier vehicle had caught the mini off-side, run it off the road and through the hedge into the ditch beyond.

"I'm a nurse," Sally volunteered in a quiet tone. "There may be someone hurt down there . . ."

"One of the passengers has gone to a house to ask if he can telephone for the ambulance and the police," the conductor said in a flat, toneless voice. "Hope the woman in the car's all right. The kid with the ball rushed off, bawling his head off. With all the playing fields and recreation grounds there are round here you'd think their mothers would have more sense than to let them play around on the edge of the road. Might have been a worse accident, might have killed the kid himself."

"I'm going down to see if there's anything I can do," Sally told him, handing him her handbag. "Look after this for me, will you? There's not much in it, too far off pay-day, but I need what there is!"

The man gave her a reassuring grin, heartened by her obvious acceptance of the accident in contrast to the behaviour of the other three passengers, who had been sitting in the downstairs part of the bus and who now stood around, wringing their hands and decrying the behaviour of the modern child and its parents. Ignoring them, Sally slid gently down the small embankment until she came to a halt beside the small car, which was lying on its side, the far part of the roof crushed inwards where it had hit the kerb. There was a woman behind the steering wheel and she appeared to be trapped by the shoulder. Her eyes were closed in her white face, and there was blood trickling down the sleeve of her linen suit. Obviously she had been cut by splinters of the broken windscreen which had crumbled into a thousand small pieces with the force of the impact on the kerb. It was with a sense of horror but not, she was astonished to realise, surprise, that Sally recognised the woman in the car as Mrs. Curtis Anderby Palmer, mother of *her* Curtis Palmer, surgeon at the General.

Carefully Sally slid her hand through the shattered window of the car, breathing a silent prayer of gratitude to whoever it was who had invented the thick, special glass which would splinter but not break. As though she sensed approaching help, Mrs. Palmer moaned slightly and, with an obvious effort, opened her eyes. They were, Sally saw, the same shade of grey-blue as were her son's, and, seeing her at such close quarters, Sally knew now how very much like his mother Curtis really was.

"Nurse?" she questioned feebly, so that Sally had to strain to hear. "You are the nurse, aren't you? The one Curtis is always talking about?"

"I am a nurse, yes," Sally told her, colour rising in her face as she realised just what Mrs. Palmer had said about Curtis. "I'm Sally Nesbitt, and I work at the General. Keep quite still," she admonished, as Mrs. Palmer showed signs of trying to move. "The ambulance will be here in a minute or so, and the men will be able to lift you out, then we can see where you're really hurt."

"It's my shoulder." Mrs. Palmer's voice was a little

stronger and Sally could guess from whom Curtis derived some of his strong determination. "I think it's fractured. I was once a nurse too," she said with a sudden sweet smile exactly like that of her son, then, as she moved again, a fresh bout of pain shot cruel fingers into her and, mercifully, she lost consciousness.

She was still unconscious when the ambulance arrived, the police car hot on their heels. Sally stood by, helping where and how she could, as the men first removed the door of the car and then gently and capably lifted Mrs. Palmer from behind the steering wheel and on to the stretcher with its folded red blanket. Just for a moment her eyes fluttered open again and the hand of her un-injured arm reached out.

"Come with me, Nurse, *please*," she begged.

Sally did not hesitate. She had been talking to the policeman, who had asked how much she had witnessed of what had happened.

"Have you finished with me now?" she asked. "I've told you all I can."

"You've been very helpful, miss," the man told her. "Thank you very much. You'll probably be called as a witness. That be all right?"

"Of course," Sally said, giving the driver of the bus a friendly smile. He had looked so worried when the police arrived that Sally had been particularly scrupulous in her account of what had happened, realising the effort the man had made to try and avoid both the child and the mini.

"Thank goodness the child was all right," she said to him as she prepared to board the ambulance. "I think you were marvellous, avoiding him the way you did."

"The child," said the policeman in a disgusted tone, "ought to be spanked for playing with a ball there and for diving after it into the road. The hours I spend going round the schools drilling road safety into them, and then the first time a favourite toy is in danger, all you've ever told 'em is forgotten! It's the mothers who are to blame in part. Some towns haven't playing facilities, but they haven't that excuse here." He was still grumbling to himself as Sally boarded the ambulance and took a seat beside Mrs. Palmer, who at once reached out for her hand.

"Curtis talks about you a great deal," she said in a tired voice. "You're a wonderful nurse. Pity you have a serious boy friend already."

"But I haven't." The words were out before Sally realised she should have been soothing and quieting her patient, not saying anything which might cause her to worry. "That is . . . Mike Amberton, the reporter, and I are good friends, we've been friends a long time, but it's nothing more than that . . ."

Mrs. Palmer's eyes opened wide and she was about to say something else, but at that moment the ambulance halted in the courtyard of the General, the doors were opened and two nurses from Casualty were there to take charge of the stretcher.

"Stay with me, Sally . . . as long as you can," Mrs. Palmer whispered, and Sally nodded, walking alongside the stretcher as her companion was wheeled away to the X-ray room.

"I'll wait," she promised as they vanished inside, but the moment the two cadet nurses were free she took one of them by the arm.

"Remember me?" she queried. "Staff Nurse Nesbitt." And receiving the affirmative nod she hurried on, "Go and find Mr. Palmer, and tell him his mother has been involved in an accident. Don't say anything to get him worried," she cautioned, "just tell him what I've told you to say. Ask him to try and be here by the time she has been X-rayed."

"Is—is she his mother?" the cadet asked in awed tones, and Sally smiled, not reproving her, because she realised the girl had a 'crush' on Curtis, as so many of them did.

"Yes," she said briefly, "she is, and they're devoted. Now, scoot, and don't have him scared to death with anxiety."

Curtis could not have been very tangled up at that moment, for he was with Sally a few moments before his mother was wheeled out of the X-ray theatre. His face was white under his tan, and there was fear in the glance he sent anxiously in Sally's direction.

'How strange,' she thought, 'we deal with this sort of thing every day, and when it comes home to us we're as worried as the rest.'

"Sally, Cadet Bowser said Mother was hurt."

"She is, I'm afraid." Sally spoke calmly, evenly, her tone conveying there was no immediate need for anxiety. "I don't think it's anything serious," she ventured, "but it will be painful. Her shoulder was trapped, her arm cut, but she was conscious and there appeared to be no head injuries. She . . . talked to me," she ended, colour flooding her face again as she remembered what Mrs. Palmer had said, "and she was quite sensible, fully aware of what she was saying all the time."

"Thank God for that," Curtis said fervently. "What happened, do you know?"

Briefly Sally gave him an account of the accident, and she had just finished telling him all about it when Mrs. Palmer was wheeled out to join them. Immediately Curtis excused himself to Sally and went to his mother's side, leaving her after a moment to consult with the radiographer. He returned to Sally after a moment or two's conversation, a smile back in his eyes and on his lips.

"Fractured shoulder," he reported, "broken arm and a fairly deep cut. She's been lucky. I shall look after her myself, in a few moments when I've scrubbed up." He eyed Sally for a moment then added unexpectedly: "I wish you could have been on theatre duty, Sally, but——"

"I can do it," Sally offered, "but I'd like to make a telephone call first."

"It doesn't matter." The smile was gone. "It would be asking a little too much. Matron has been very kind about you staying so long with Francie. We mustn't expect her to fit in with all personal requests."

"I'd like to help." Sally felt she must persist. "Would you care for me to go and ask Matron?" she added, and hoped he did not guess how the thought of putting such a request made her tremble. But he shook his head, smiling at her again and laying a hand on her arm, unknowingly sending what seemed to be millions of electric sparks coursing through her pulses.

"No. No, thank you," he said quietly. "Come and see Mother while she's convalescing. I shall take her home with me tonight, if Matron agrees. She won't require much nursing care, simply rest and quiet until she's over the shock, but she'll get awfully bored, unable to use her arm properly for a while, and anyway," he ended boyishly, "she'd love you to come."

"I will, then," Sally promised. "I'll call as soon as I'm able."

He was gone then, striding away from her to scrub up before performing the operation on his mother. Mrs Palmer was wheeled away, smiling bravely at Sally as she went, and then she was free to go on her way, much later than she had planned, to her meeting with Mike and the others.

She had some time to wait for another bus, and when she finally caught one it was to discover the town crowded, as she had expected, with mothers and children.

'Tea first,' she told herself, giving up altogether the idea of the prolonged shopping spree to which she had been looking forward all day. 'Then just the essentials and off to the Blue Grill.'

She chose a small, select tea-shop, but even this had been invaded today by mothers and their offspring, and it was some time before Sally's modest order was attended to. She could not linger long over her meal, or she would have had no time at all in which to shop, but at last she was free, out in the streets again and heading for the multiple store where she was fairly certain of being able to match the silks for the embroidery which was her hobby.

Sally was just turning the corner into Trafford Street where the store was situated, when someone took her almost violently by the arm, halting her progress.

"Nurse . . . Nurse Nesbitt, that's it, isn't it?" a voice demanded, and she found herself looking up into the brilliant gaze of Martin Howbury.

"Yes," she said quietly, aware that for some reason his

eyes were literally blazing with fury and that the little muscles at the corners of his mouth were working over-time. "Is there something wrong?" she asked.

"There certainly is," he said, so briefly that Sally with-drew a little, feeling herself shrink from his anger as he propelled her by the arm into the doorway of a nearby shop, away from the bustling crowds on the pavement. "I don't even know whether you can help or not," Martin rushed on, "but it's worth a try. I admired your integrity when you came to the office, and I have an instinctive feeling I can trust you, that you'll tell me the truth and help if you can."

"I certainly will help, as you say, if I can," Sally told him. "Perhaps if you explained what this is all about?"

"Have you seen Mavis Trane?" was the next, totally unexpected question. Sally shook her head.

"Not for a long time," she said slowly, remembering that she had last seen the girl when she had been report-ing the children's fancy dress dance, round about February. "Certainly not today. Why?"

"It doesn't matter." The brilliant dark brown eyes looked straight into Sally's sherry-brown ones with the most penetrating glance she had ever encountered. "You say you haven't seen her 'for a long time'," he quoted. "You're still up at Queen's Close, aren't you?"

"Yes," Sally said, mystified, "but I don't think I shall be there very much longer. Miss Francie is so much better, practically as good as new." She ventured a smile, but it was not returned.

"Has Mavis Trane been there too?" he asked next. "Has she visited, do you know?"

"I haven't seen her," Sally said truthfully. "What *is* all this? What has Mavis Trane to do with Queen's Close or with me?"

"Nothing, I hope," Martin snapped. "If you *do* see her—she's running around town today getting pictures of the swimming gala at the Old Baths—tell her to report to me as soon as she gets back to the office, and tell her too that unless she has some excellent and reasonable explana-tion for what she has in her column today, then she's sacked, and I don't care how good a columnist she might be."

"But . . ." Sally was beginning, when someone opened the door of the shop behind her and a number of people, all of a family, it appeared, streamed out and on to the pavement, cutting off the conversation. From the kerbside Martin looked across at her, giving her a half-salute.

"Read it for yourself, Nurse," he suggested. "Maybe you'll be able to think of a way to help me after you've read it."

"I will," Sally promised, "and," she added rashly, since she had absolutely no idea of what she might be letting herself in for, "I'll help if I can."

"Thanks." Martin's face lightened. "I believe you. 'Bye." The next minute he was off, striding down the street and Sally turned to enter the store and buy her silks, puzzled and more than a little uneasy. Whatever it was it had apparently upset Martin Howbury more than a little, so whatever it was must be something concerning Francie Bodman.

'And if he didn't care, as much as Francie says he cares, then he wouldn't be getting all worked up about it,' Sally reasoned to herself. 'I must buy an evening paper.'

She bought one from the little old man standing on the next corner, but she had no time to read it just then. A glance at her watch told her that the others would already be at the Blue Grill Room and would be waiting for her, and Mike at any rate would be certain something dreadful had happened to make her late, for since she had first met him and known how important time was to him, she had always made a point of being punctual for their meetings, even though it was often Mike who was delayed by a previous appointment and she was the one kept waiting.

She hurried as fast as she could along the packed streets and at last she arrived at the Blue Grill Room. Mike's car and Peter's were both parked outside, and Sally quickened her steps, worrying a little because it was obvious they had been there some time, wedged in as they were by cars on either side.

"Hello." Mike's friendly face lit up with his customary smile as he saw her approaching. "I've ordered yours. Wherever have you been?" he demanded all in one breath as he pushed a glass into her hand. "I've been imagining all sorts of things, possible and—I hope—impossible."

"I got involved. I mean I witnessed an accident, and I had to help." Sally told the truth, but did not add to whom the accident had happened or any further details. "I was kept a time at the hospital," she explained, "and then there were crowds of people in the tea-room and it took ages to get served. Then I met Martin Howbury..."

"And you had to talk to him about your precious Francesca, I know," Mike grinned. "Did he tell you his book's been accepted by a leading publisher and that his agent has a film company wanting to buy the film rights as well?"

"No, he didn't." Sally was genuinely surprised. "He was upset. You haven't seen Mavis Trane around, have you?" she added. "He's furious about something she's written in her page today, and he wants me to help him. I don't know how."

"What's she written?" Mike demanded, pulling a paper from under his arm. "I've been rushed off my feet all day, but so far as I knew she was reporting the swimming gala at the Old Baths."

"That's what Martin said," Sally told him, "so it must have been something she reported in time for today's press. Surely the results of the gala will appear in to-morrow's edition?"

"Who cares *when* they appear, except the parents of the kids doing the swimming?" Pete demanded plaintively, sweeping the paper aside and off the bar counter. "Look at your bally paper in a minute. We came here to celebrate. Aren't you going to drink to us, Sally?"

"Sorry." Sally laughed at his outraged expression. "We can look at the paper in a minute. What are we drinking?"

"Champagne cocktails," Pete announced triumphantly. "What else?" and he gave the necessary order. Shyly

Betty held out her left hand, her usually pert little face serious and grave.

"Do you like it, Sally?" she asked tentatively. "We chose it together. I'm Cancer, you see, so we chose emeralds . . . my birthstone."

"It's beautiful," Sally said sincerely, dutifully admiring the square-cut emerald with its circle of small diamonds. "And I'm sure you're both going to be very, very happy."

"Let's drink to that," Mike suggested, lifting his glass, and as she responded to the toast Sally's glance met his and her heart felt suddenly cold, as if all the sunshine had gone from the day, because before she left him that evening she was determined to tell Mike the truth, to advise him to find someone else, and cut herself off from one of the nicest people she had known in her life.

CHAPTER SIXTEEN

THEY sat chatting and enjoying their drinks and the varied cocktail snacks at the bar, and when Mike wanted to pay for another round for the four of them, Pete waved his hand in a magnificent gesture which would have been funny had he not worn such a grave, almost stern expression.

"This is on me," he announced seriously. "This is *our* celebration, Betty's and mine, and you," he included both Sally and Mike in one sweeping gesture, "are our honoured guests. Same again?"

"Are you two coming to the cinema with us?" Betty asked, as the fresh drinks were brought. "It's not much of a way to celebrate, but Pete's on duty tonight and I haven't a late pass."

"I don't want to be late in either," Sally said quickly, and was aware of the quick glance Mike gave her before he, too, answered Betty's invitation.

"I want to look in on the cricket match at the Green," he said. "They like the latest scores 'at the time of going to press'. It may not be county cricket, but most folks locally are interested. I've a big day tomorrow, as well, so I think you ought to go off on your own. After all, as Pete pointed out, this is your celebration. It ought to be just the two of you."

"If you can't you can't, and that's all there is to it," Betty remarked philosophically. "Pass me your paper, Mike, and let's see what's on everywhere, please."

"I've got a paper, too." Sally took hers from under her arm and spread it out on the counter. "You two look at the cinema announcements, and Mike and I will try to find out what it is that's upsetting Martin Howbury so much."

She folded the paper to Mavis Trane's page, and for a moment she and Mike studied the print in silence, then Mike smothered an exclamation and pointed with his finger. Sally looked where he pointed. Under the small, heavy-type printing of the paragraph's heading she read:

"Wedding bells? I wonder. It is rumoured that a certain leading surgeon of the town is contemplating a proposal of marriage to the town's charming and wealthy heiress who has been under his care. We understand the young lady in question is now almost well again, but perhaps still in need of . . . medical care and attention?"

"I don't believe it." Sally's small, heart-shaped face was so white that Mike looked anxiously at her, wondering if she were about to faint. There was stark incredulity in the sherry-brown eyes and her lower lip had started to tremble in a childish fashion as if she were about to burst into tears. "She—she was talking about Martin before I left," Sally said, a sudden wild hope in her heart. "She said she'd make him change his mind . . . Do you think . . . ?"

"I don't think anything," Mike said cryptically, "not about this"—he tapped the paper with an impatient finger—"that is. If she is responsible for this in an endeavour to attract Martin's attention, then all I can say is she's chosen a queer way to attract him." He eyed Sally closely. He was far more concerned with the effect the announcement had had upon Sally than with anything concerning either Francie or Martin Howbury just then. "Sally," he said in the direct way she knew so well, "it . . . meant something to you, didn't it? Reading what Mavis has written about Francie and Curtis Palmer, I mean."

"Yes. Yes, it did." Sally knew the moment had come when she could no longer avoid telling Mike the truth. "It meant . . . everything to me."

"You said," Mike countered in a tone that was almost an accusation, "you would tell me if ever you found . . . anyone else."

"But I haven't," Sally told him quietly. "That is . . . he, Curtis Palmer, doesn't see any woman *as* a woman. Francie said this yesterday. She said he had told her he only thought of her as 'an interesting case'. That's how he sees everyone . . . as a nurse or as a patient. It's difficult to explain . . ." She broke off nervously.

With a decisive movement Mike suddenly folded the paper neatly and tucked it under his arm.

"Let's get out of here," he suggested quietly. "Somewhere where we can talk." He gave a glance at Betty and Pete, still scanning the lists of entertainment to be had that evening. "If you two have no objections," he said in an even tone, "we'll be running along. The light's going, it'll be 'close of play' before we know where we are . . . and we think you'll enjoy the pictures better on your own," he ended with a mischievous twinkle in his eyes.

"If you're sure . . ."? Betty began, looking questioningly at Sally, who managed to smile and nod. She did not intend any worries about her private affairs to spoil the celebration evening for her friend.

"I want to get in early," she said in a small voice, and wondered how she was going to face Francie until she knew the true story of what lay behind Mavis Trane's gossip column.

"I'll give you a ring," Betty told her, "as soon as we've made any plans."

"Right." Sally smiled. "I may be back at the General any time now, then we can talk things over," she ended. They exchanged a few more remarks about the plans Betty and Pete had tentatively made, but Mike was moving restlessly and had twice glanced at his watch, so that Sally thought it wiser to cut the conversation short.

"Where shall we go?" she asked him as they left the Blue Grill Room. "The Copper Bowl?"

"No," Mike said definitely. "I don't want to be . . . shut in. Let's drive out towards the green. I can call in there and find out the scores at close of play and then go on to Sandygate Lane. We can park there and talk for a while. Nobody will disturb us." Sally looked up into Mike's—for once—serious face, a troubled little frown between her brows.

"I . . . it won't do any good, Mike," she said gently. Mike gave her a wry smile and tucked her hand under his arm in just the way he usually did.

"Let me be the best judge of that, if you don't mind," he suggested. "So far as I'm concerned, no time spent in your company is ever wasted. Now, come along."

They did not talk as they sped along the road leading to the playing fields and after that, the open country. Sally felt she must wait for Mike's lead. He knew her so well that he must have known what she meant when she had said it wouldn't be any good talking together, and the ache in her heart began all over again, so that she began to wonder if, after all, it would not be better to go on as they had done all the time they had known one another, going around together when their free time coincided, telephoning, chatting . . . but, she told herself in a last spurt of fairness, with all the real 'caring' on Mike's side only.

"I won't be a minute." Sally shut off her thoughts with a start as she realised they had reached the gates of the cricket enclosure. She smiled at him and sat quietly watching as he went hurrying along with the peculiar long, rapid stride which, when they were together, he tried in vain to match up to her shorter, more feminine steps.

'It wouldn't be fair,' she told herself seriously, 'to ask him to go on in this way any longer, not now that I *know* it will never be any different for me. It wasn't so unfair before I *was* certain . . . now I ought to let Mike find

someone else.' But the thought of someone else rushing
hither and thither with Mike, sitting beside him in his
little car, having the right to call him on the phone to
make or cancel an arrangement, brought little comfort to
her heart. It was only stern resolve which made her mentally stick to her decision to make an end of things tonight, no matter what he said.

"Next stop Sandygate Lane," Mike announced cheerfully, slipping into the driving seat and pulling a package
from his pocket. "Mary Robertson had brought a picnic
and then been too busy to have it. I've accepted the
crisps and the coffee. Want me to go back for anything
else?"

"No, thanks." Sally had to smile. No matter how busy
he was, how full his day, Mike always made time to eat.
And that might help, she decided wryly. Nobody could
possibly try to become romantic while occupied in dispos-
ing of coffee and crisps!

Mike drew the car into the side of the roadway of the
little leafy lane. It was a place where they had sometimes
parked before, perhaps after a cricket match Mike had
been reporting, perhaps on their way back to Barcaster
from some out-of-town visit.

"Well?" Mike began, one arm across the seat and
behind her, but carefully not touching her. "Where do we
go from here?"

"I . . . I don't quite know," Sally told him honestly. "I
. . . that is, I know what we ought to do," she ended
lamely.

The corners of Mike's mobile mouth lifted a little and
there was a strange expression in his eyes as he looked at
her. It seemed he was smiling at her in an indulgent way,
as one might smile at a dearly loved child which was
intent upon going its own way, and yet there was a hint
of sadness, as though he were already saying goodbye to
her and to the happy times they had known together, as
though, Sally thought suddenly, he had already accepted
defeat. The thought saddened her, but she knew that in
order to be fair to him she had to make the break,
whether he would or not.

"And . . . what is that, Sally?" he asked, as though he were determined not to help her.

"We ought to . . . not say goodbye, exactly," Sally floundered, "but . . . stop seeing each other. It's not fair to you, and it's going to be difficult to avoid each other in a small town like Barcaster, when we both know so many of the same people, go to so many of the same places." She paused, because Mike was still looking at her in the same quizzical way.

"Well, what would you have us do?" he asked seriously. "Any ideas?"

"Yes." Sally took her courage in both hands. Mike, she knew, was ambitious, but not overwhelmingly so. "Ask for a transfer," she suggested. "There are bigger papers—of your own firm—in Milcaster. You could still get home to see your folks at weekends, and you'd maybe get a step up the ladder too," she ended abruptly.

"And . . ." Mike mimicked her gently, "maybe I'll meet some other girl to take around with me, someone who'll laugh at the same jokes, like the same shows—or pretend she does—someone whose steps will fit mine when we're dancing . . . that's what you're hoping, isn't it, Sally?"

"It . . . it would be a good thing for you if you did," she answered, stubbornly sticking to her point.

Mike suddenly took his arm from the back of the seat and laid his hand gently on hers where they lay, clasped in her lap.

"And you, Sally," he said gently, "what will *you* do? Go on nursing, working alongside a man who only sees the uniform and not the girl inside it? Who won't know whether you're feeling on top of the world or under the weather, and if he knows, will just accept that 'Nurse is off colour today' and leave it at that, not worry because it isn't just 'Nurse' who's not feeling well, it's Sally, Sally who deserves to be loved and cosseted and taken care of, and who likes to do all that for other people but never has it done for her. Will that be your life, Sally, until you're too old and too tired to do it any longer?"

"I don't know," Sally said miserably. "You make it all

sound . . . very dreary . . . but"—she made herself say
the words because they *had* to be said, and Mike certainly
wasn't helping her—"it isn't fair to you. You're husband
material, Mike," she said, giving him one of his own
quotes, smiling a little as she did so. "You're the type who
makes a good husband, and you deserve a good wife, not
one who can't give you back the kind of love you ought
to have, the whole of her love."

"I'd be satisfied to have a part," Mike said doggedly,
but Sally shook her head.

"Not after a time, you wouldn't," she told him with a
wisdom beyond her years. "You think now that you
would, but when the newness had worn off, when we
became a settled, married couple, you'd want a family,
and you'd want—and have every right to expect—that
family to have the right background, a background firm
and true, not founded on compromise."

"I expect you're right." Mike gave her hands a friendly,
firm pressure as though in farewell, and removed his own.
"I *know* you're right," he went on, "but I'm foolish
enough to dislike knowing I'm wrong in trying to per-
suade you to change your mind. I'll take your advice,
Sally love"—he twisted round in his seat so that she
could not look directly into his face—"but I'm going to
tell you something I want you always to remember. I'm
quite prepared to admit there may be some other girl
who'll . . . do. I'm not so foolish as to believe I'd always
be content to go through life without anyone. It's out of
fashion now for men to go off big-game hunting if they've
been . . . crossed in love, is the phrase, I believe, and
anyhow, I couldn't afford either the time or the money.
But," and suddenly there was a more serious note in his
voice than she had ever heard from him before, "one
thing that hasn't gone out of fashion so far as I'm concerned is faithfulness."

He paused for so long that Sally thought he had
finished, but just as she was about to comment he spoke
again.

"I shall always love you, Sally, no matter whether I
marry someone else or not. That doesn't mean I shall

marry someone I don't or can't love, but it will never again be the same feeling I have for you. That only comes once in a lifetime . . . or so I say now. Maybe time will prove me wrong, we shall see. But whatever happens, I want you to know that, if you need me, or if I think you need me or that I can help you, I shall be there."

There were no heroics, no false drama was attached to the statement, for that was all it was, a plain statement of a fact he wished her to become aware of and to remember.

"Never forget that, Sally," he cautioned her. "If ever you need someone to help you, advise you if they can, a shoulder to cry on"—there was a sudden wry twist to his lips—"or . . . anything of that nature, I shall deem it an insult if you fail to let me know. Promise?"

"I . . . promise," Sally said in a small, shaky voice. She felt strangely humbled by Mike's words, and as though she had not known before, she suddenly felt she had never appreciated just how deeply he did care, just what their friendship had meant to him and just how deeply he must be hurt at this moment. It was, she decided as the realisation hit her, only fair to end it as quickly as possible.

"I'm . . . proud to have been your . . . friend all this time," she managed slowly. "You say big-game hunting for men isn't in fashion any more. That answers your question to me about what I'm going to do from now on. Yes," she was answering what he had asked much earlier and they both realised it, "I shall go on . . . working at the General, doing the best I can to help people in pain and sickness, working sometimes with one doctor, sometimes with another. But"—the small chin lifted proudly—"going into a decline or whatever it was called in the Victorian times isn't in fashion for girls any more than is big-game hunting for you. I shall find *my* comfort in my work."

"You don't think *you* could . . . find someone else, then?" Mike asked the question, but unhopefully, as though he were already sure of the answer. Sally shook her head.

"If . . . anyone else would have . . . done," she said with a faint smile as she quoted him, "although that isn't a very nice way to put it, the 'someone else' would have been *you*, Mike, and you know it. No, my dear, let's leave it at that and say goodbye before we spoil all that's gone before."

"Nothing could do that," Mike said firmly, "but we won't say goodbye, just cheerio. That leaves it open, just in case," he added, leaning forward and switching on the engine. The car leapt into life as he turned to face her. "Want to go back to Queen's Close now?" he asked her quietly.

"Please." And again she thought how well he knew her, how great was his understanding.

There didn't appear to be anything else left to say. Sally sat quietly beside Mike as the miles sped past, thinking over all the happy times they had enjoyed together and already half regretting that she had felt compelled to put an end to it all. By the time Mike had turned the car in at the entrance to the huge old house the tears were not far away.

Mike saw this as he pulled up at the foot of the flight of stone steps leading to the entrance, and there was tenderness in his glance as he looked down on her small, erect figure.

"Let me prescribe for you tonight, Sally love," he suggested in much the same tone her brother might have used in the same or similar circumstances. "If you can get up to bed without having to talk to anyone I should do so, and if you can't, say you've a headache or something and cut along as fast as you can. Don't let all this worry you. I wish things could have worked out right for one of us . . . they couldn't for us both, and if it had to be just one I'd rather it could have been for you. Let me kiss you . . . this way, just once . . ." And before Sally could protest he had stooped and gathered her into his arms, his lips coming down firmly on her own.

For a moment Sally stood passive in his embrace, and as the headlights of another car coming up the drive shone upon them she made an effort and pulled herself away, just as the other car halted and she saw the caller was Curtis.

Sally had no means of knowing whether he had seen the embrace or not. He did not appear to have eyes for either of them, not speaking, but swinging himself out of the car and walking briskly along towards the pool, where lanterns had been hung round the water's edge and where, in the dim light, Francie could be seen on the garden lounging chair.

"Thanks for the memory," Mike said quietly, getting into his own car, "and don't forget our exchange of promises. Cheerio, little Sally, take care of yourself." And in a moment he was gone.

Sally stood where she was, watching until the lights of his car disappeared. It gave her a strange, lonely feeling to realise that, of her own accord, she had sent Mike out of her life for ever. From the pool came the sound of voices, and there appeared to be an argument, but suddenly Sally was too tired to care. She turned and went listlessly indoors, intent only upon taking Mike's advice and retiring to bed as speedily as she could.

In the hall she encountered old Sam, who appeared to be busily engaged in trimming one of the numerous pot plants which stood about. In an abstracted way Sally felt he was waiting for something, but she was too tired to wonder what it might be.

"Will you please make my excuses to the others, Mr. Bodman?" she asked him quietly as he greeted her. "I've —a headache. I'm going straight to bed."

"Very wise, my dear, very wise." The old gentleman nodded his head as if in self-agreement. "I hope you'll find it better by morning . . . most things are," he added inconsequently. "Goodnight."

CHAPTER SEVENTEEN

SALLY went slowly up the beautiful staircase and into her own room, drawing the curtains before she put on the light, remembering that from certain angles round the pool her room window was visible and somehow, as yet, not anxious to see Francie until she had had some time alone to think out the possible explanation of the paragraph in Mavis Trane's page.

She sat down on the comfortable easy-chair thoughtfully provided, and lit a cigarette, half inclined to close her open window, but the murmur of the voices below was so quiet as to render the words uttered undistinguishable, and she remained where she was, half thinking of Mike, now on his lonely way back to Barcaster, and half still worrying about Francie and Curtis and what the gossip paragraph had implied.

'Francie told me herself that Curtis said she meant no more to him than being an interesting patient,' she reminded herself sternly. 'Why should she lie?'

Her thoughts turned back to when she had last seen Curtis—before the fleeting glimpse of a few moments ago—and he had been striding away from her on his way to prepare himself for the small operation on his mother.

'I wonder how she is,' Sally thought inconsequently. 'And I wonder if he meant it when he asked me to go and see her?'

She got up from the chair and began to pace the room. If only she could go away. Betty would soon be leaving the General, and although Sally had many other friends among the nurses there, none of them was as close, as intimate, as Betty and she had always been.

'I could go abroad,' she mused, but she knew she would not. She would do what she had told Mike she would do, stay on at the General, seeing Curtis every day, feeling the knife twist in her heart and, she stopped her pacing, appalled at the sudden thought which had assailed her, perhaps, in the future, one day see him really fall in love with someone else, maybe some other nurse or Sister, and then she would experience the greater agony of knowing him to be there but no longer walking alone, belonging to someone else.

'I ought to go,' she told herself, but without much real belief that she ever would. ' I ought to clear out, while it doesn't hurt too much,' but she knew she would stay, knew that she would always hope that something would happen to make her a person so far as Curtis Palmer was concerned. She remembered what his mother had said ... that it was a pity she had a serious boy friend.

'But I told her I hadn't,' Sally remembered. 'I wonder if she told *him,* or if the pain in her shoulder made her forget, or ...'

It was at this point in her thoughts that she heard the other car coming up the drive. Sally had been well trained by her brother, and she knew at once by the sound of the engine that this was not a car belonging to the inhabitants of Queen's Close, or of any of those who were accustomed to visiting there. The engine stopped, the door of the car slammed, then quick masculine footsteps sounded loudly on the terrace. There was the sound too, of a man's voice, but although she strained her ears Sally could not hear what was said nor could she place the speaker, although there seemed to be something familiar in the sound of the voice. What she did hear was Ivy's clear voice, with its extraordinary power of being carried without seeming to shout, inform the unknown visitor that 'Miss Francie is by the bathing pool. I shall be coming to help her indoors very soon, sir', then the footsteps sounded again.

For no known reason Sally found her pulses were racing and that she was holding herself alert, as though some danger threatened her patient and she should be there to help.

'Don't be an ass,' she cautioned herself. 'It's obviously someone who knows her well, and Curtis is there.' But all the same, she continued to listen intently.

For a moment or so she heard nothing further, then,

on the still air, came the sound of a man's voice raised in anger. With a sense of shock Sally shook herself as she realised the voice, the quick, impatient footsteps and therefore obviously the strange car, belonged to Martin Howbury.

'He's come to see Francie . . . to have it out with her. He'll be furious when he finds Curtis there too,' she told herself.

From the pool came the sound of another voice, another masculine voice, also raised in anger, and this time there was no mistaking the crisp, cool authoritative tones of Curtis Palmer. Sally had heard him speak thus too often in the hospital to be in any doubt.

'I ought to go down,' she told herself, and yet what business was it of hers? She had no right to interfere in whatever was taking place by the bathing pool. She was only in this house as Francie's nurse, not for any other reason. A moment or so later her doubts were routed, as, rising over the voices of the two men, came the sound of Francie crying.

'I *am* going down,' she told herself fiercely. 'Francie will upset herself if she carries on like this.'

She snapped off the light and caught up her coat, which she had thrown on to the bed when she came in, then she went quickly and quietly downstairs. Old Sam was still in the hall, fussing around his plants and humming softly to himself. Sally gave him a quick glance. For someone who was supposed to have the welfare of his granddaughter so close to his heart, he appeared to be quite undisturbed by the sounds which reached them unmistakably here. Sally hurried on until she came down to the pool itself. Francie was still half sitting, half reclining on the lounging chair, and Curtis had obviously risen from the deck-chair by her side. Opposite them, his unruly hair more awry than ever, his brilliant dark eyes alight with anger visible even in the dim light of the swinging lanterns, Martin faced them, his whole attitude a challenge.

"What am I to believe?" he was asking as Sally neared the pool and yet remained unseen, unobserved, in the shadow of a weeping willow tree. "You said . . ." He seemed to choke on the next words as he swung round to face Francie directly. "You said you'd let me know if there ever was anyone else. You also said there never *would* be anyone else. You let me think you wandered on to the parapet to think things out, to see what was best to do to help us, that's what you said," he went on ruthlessly, "and yet, not six months after all this, after we've all been so worried about you, and after I've nearly driven myself mad, wondering if I were guilty, if I ought to have given way, buried my pride, there's . . . this"— his finger stabbed the paper in his hand—"in Mavis Trane's page. How it got past me and down into the compositor's room I'll never know. I *will* know," he corrected himself without pausing for breath. "I shan't rest until I *do* know. How much of this did you hint to her, Francie? How much did you leave to her to make up herself?"

"I haven't seen her," Francie said tearfully. "I don't even *know* her. I've never spoken to her in my life. The only thing I've had to do with Mavis Trane . . ."

She paused, and from where she was Sally could just see the other girl was biting her lip in the nervous way she had when she was worried or upset in any way.

"Yes?" Martin seemed to shoot the one word at her, it was uttered in such an explosive fashion. "The only thing you've had to do with Mavis Trane is *what*?" he demanded. "If you don't know her, how can you have had anything to do with her?"

"It was when you sent those flowers to me . . . the ones in the hospital, after Sally had been to see you." The words were halting, spoken in almost a whisper. "I asked Sally if she knew anything about the language of flowers. I knew you'd written something about it in one of your books . . . you told me, remember?"

"Yes. Go on," Martin said, but there was a new gentleness in his voice which was not lost on Sally.

"Sally said she knew nothing about it, but she telephoned her friend—you know who I mean, Mike somebody, a reporter."

"Mike Amberton, yes," Martin prodded impatiently. "What did *he* say, and where does Mavis come into all this?"

"I don't know what Mike said," Francie answered with a little more spirit than she had so far displayed, and Sally could have hugged her for it, "but I think he put her through to Mavis Trane, and she looked up the meanings for us."

"Did she know who was making the enquiry and why?" Martin asked next. Francie shook her head.

"I don't know," she said slowly. "I shouldn't think so. Sally didn't say. She just told me the . . . meanings of the flowers."

"I see." Suddenly there didn't appear to be anything more to say, and Sally thought Martin was about to turn away and leave Curtis and Francie alone together, but at the last moment he turned, his brilliant dark eyes searching Francie's face with a glance so deep, so full of yearning, that instinctively Sally's generous heart went out to him. He *did* love Francie, she was convinced of that, he loved her as Mike loved Sally, and all that love was there for her to see for herself, if she would.

"I've got to say it, Francie." His voice was suddenly hoarse and yet quiet, no longer shouting and full of charged emotion. "I swore—both to you and myself— that I'd never say this, but I *have* to. I don't know yet what I'm going to make of my last book. I have a feeling the film company will take it, make a picture of it, and that it will make a good one. By that"—his mouth twisted wryly—"I mean a popular one. That will help the book. Somehow the feeling persists, but I've no grounds for it, just a hunch, and I wouldn't normally stake your future on a hunch, but if you will, Francie, if you'll promise to manage on what I make, whether this book is the success I hope for or not, if you'll promise not to try and . . . buy me . . . or to let your family try and buy me . . . then . . ." He did not move or take even one step towards her, but something seemed to the watching Sally to leap between them, some invisible yet tangible current of emotion so strong that she could feel its effects where she stood. "Will

F

you . . . marry me, Francie?" he asked, quietly, humbly. "Will you marry me . . . soon?"

"As soon as I can!" She had left where she stood and, for the first time since her accident, she was running, scorning the stick which lay beside the lounging chair. She ran across the smooth turf and into Martin's waiting arms.

Sally glanced at Curtis. His face was hidden by the shadows, but she saw him square his shoulders, move slightly and then resume his former position. In the quietness which had followed Francie's answer to Martin's proposal, his voice sounded louder than usual.

"Well, if Francie wasn't responsible for the piece of nonsense in the gossip column, I should like to know who was," he said crisply. "I'm also involved, you may remember."

Martin turned to him as though he had just become aware of his presence, but Sally knew that was not the case.

"You may rest assured I shall find out who and why," Martin said quietly, "but right now, since whoever did it has solved a problem for Francie and myself, I'm not too concerned."

"But I am." Curtis sounded angry, Sally decided, then he added: "Allow me to be the first to offer you both my sincere congratulations . . ." And suddenly Sally could bear no more. Her heart ached for him, not knowing, not really caring, whether his emotions had been involved or not. Whether that was the case or whether his interest in Francie had been, as Betty suggested, a means to gain extra advantages for the General, she neither knew nor cared. All Sally could think of at that moment was that Curtis stood alone, whether that was his desire or not, and the other two were where they should have been long ago, safely in each other's arms. She could not bear to feel he had been defeated, and yet a small part of her heart rejoiced that he was still free. Noiselessly she crept away from the garden and went back into the house, and in the hall she found old Sam, so obviously waiting that she halted and looked directly at him, meeting the penetrating glance of the shrewd blue eyes with her own level one.

"What's going on out there?" Sam demanded. "I shall go and see for myself if somebody doesn't come and tell me something soon."

"I think," Sally said in a level tone, "that your grand-daughter and your editor will soon be coming indoors to ask your blessing, maybe your help—not financially but emotionally, protection from the family and all that sort of thing—unless I'm very much mistaken."

"Good! Excellent!" There was no mistaking Sam's delight. His eyes sparkled, the corners of his mouth turned up, and he rubbed his hands briskly together before taking Sally by the elbow and leading her into the deserted dining-room. "It worked, then?" he half-questioned glee-fully. "I knew it would. Nothing like a bit of healthy jealousy, subtly delivered, to bring a body up to scratch. While he was certain she would just sit here, mooning and waiting for him to make his fortune, Martin Howbury wouldn't have moved a finger to help himself. Somebody had to do it for him."

"You mean . . . you?" Sally looked at him in amaze-ment, but Sam was busily engaged in pouring out two drinks and did not notice.

"Certainly," he said quietly, handing one brimming glass to her and lifting the other in a silent toast. "I wasn't going to stand by and see my little Francie eating out her heart for any man, not even the best editor we've ever had on the paper. Neither was I going to stand by and see him throw away all he's worked for here—or hand it over to someone else—and go off to make a fresh start with some other—maybe rival—company. No." He shook his head so that the silvery frill of hair appeared to dance. "I want them both where they belong . . . here. And *how* they belong . . . together."

"Then it was you who told Mavis Trane to put that in her column?" Sally asked, and suddenly began to giggle. "What's Martin going to say when he finds out?" she wondered aloud.

"I don't think he'll be grumbling at anyone very

much." Sam took a telegram from his pocket and held it out. "This came for him this morning. It was delivered to my office by mistake, but when I opened it I knew I had to make them go to each other without financial bribes on either side. They had to know they belonged together, regardless of the rest."

"But . . ." Sally was staring at the telegram as though she were mesmerised. "This says—or am I wrong?—that Martin's agents have accepted an offer of twenty-five thousand pounds for the film rights of his book!"

"That's right," Sam nodded again, obviously as pleased as if he had arranged the entire transaction himself. "I knew he'd come rushing to Francie at once, when he knew. I wanted him to take a risk . . . to ask her first, before either of them knew."

"And he did," Sally said thankfully. Down the drive she heard the sound of Curtis's car heading from the house, and at the sound, the sadness, the restlessness, swept over her again. Impulsively she turned to the old man. "I wish I had a grandfather . . . someone like you . . . to arrange my life for me," she said, unconsciously wistful. "It must be wonderful to have someone with so much wisdom, so much knowledge of the human race, to turn to."

"Tell me, Nurse Sally," the old man invited, patting the settee beside him as he sank down on the cool leather. "Try telling me. If I can help, you know that I will."

"You can't," Sally said decisively, her momentary weakness gone, but she sat beside him just the same. "I shall have to sort myself out first." She gave a brief little laugh, brave but without real mirth. "I shall have to get back to the General and have some sound common sense and everyday living for a week or two, until I get my feet firmly on the ground again."

"It's . . . is it young Mike Amberton?" Sam asked cautiously. "I've seen you two about a great deal together, but . . ."

"Mike and I are . . . were . . . very good friends," Sally told him slowly. Suddenly she felt the need to confide in someone, not in someone like Francie, as puzzled and as hurt by her own emotions from time to time as Sally had been, but someone like Sam Bodman, who had lived a long time and who was wise and kind, and very understanding of those many years his junior. "Mike is in love with me, Mr. Bodman," she went on seriously. "He's been in love with me for a very long time."

"And you . . . you don't love him?" Sam asked after a long pause.

Sally shook her head.

"Not in the way he means, the way most people mean," she said quietly. "I love Mike in another way . . . as I love my brother. We've all been good friends, and from the beginning I got accustomed to thinking of them together."

"And now you can't think of him in any other way, hmm?" Sam's shrewd glance met her own, but there was no twinkle in his eyes this time. "You're a wise girl, Sally child," he said slowly. "You refuse to pretend what you don't really feel, and yet"—he eyed her keenly—"you're capable of a great love, of the real kind of love which the right sort of woman has for the one man in her life. I believe you've found that love now, Sally," he said slowly, not asking a question, but making a statement.

"Yes," slowly but firmly came her answer. "I *have*," she reiterated, "but there's nothing to be done about it. You see, he doesn't love me."

"I see." There was silence for a moment, and the old man reached for the bottle of sherry, but when he would have refilled her glass Sally shook her head. He refilled his own before continuing.

"Mike Amberton has a great future," he said slowly. "Not the same kind of future Martin will have, but in the newspaper field. I think a change of scene might help . . . and in Milcaster we shall soon be requiring a new editor. Len Fearnley is going to retire. There's also a smart new girl reporter, young, keen on her job, even taking classes at the local technical college to improve her work . . . Journalism and the Law or some such, I've heard. She's keen to get on, interested in everything and everybody. Passably pretty, good company." He chuckled, and suddenly leaned forward and peered intently into Sally's face. "You wouldn't be jealous, would you?" he asked, and his eyes demanded the truth.

"I wouldn't call it jealousy." Sally smiled, but there was a hint of sadness behind the smile. "I shall be . . . envious, envious of her going around with Mike, doing all the things together that we used to enjoy doing, but"— there was no sadness in the smile this time, it was perfectly sincere—"I shall be glad for Mike's sake. That's what he needs." Her laugh bubbled out suddenly, startling Sam. "I always told him he was husband material," she said.

"That's my Sally!" Sam's hand came down on her shoulder in a warm, friendly grasp. "Have you anywhere you and your friends usually meet on your off-duty evenings?" he asked.

"Various places, for our entertainment, but we usually end up at the Copper Bowl for coffee before we go back," Sally told him. "Why?"

"Never you mind why," came the surprising answer. "Just go up and do whatever you feel you ought to do before going out again. Your day off duty isn't ended yet, there's still more than a couple of hours to go, and I have some telephoning to do. Come down to me when you're ready," he said, and Sally, mystified but aware that he made no request without some good reason for having made it, rose to her feet and went off to her room without a word of protest.

CHAPTER EIGHTEEN

SALLY came back to the dining-room to find Sam placidly puffing away at his pipe, a sure sign that the old man was satisfied with the way things were going at the moment. He only smoked cigarettes when he was worried or upset, and that was, therefore, on very rare occasions. He rose, smiling, as she came into the room.

"Good girl," he said approvingly. "I think I know a

little how you're feeling tonight," he went on musingly. "Francie has her man, and you've just said goodbye to your friend, proving yourself stronger than the temptation to hang on to someone you may hurt in the long run, and that takes a great deal of courage, especially when you're witness to someone else being as happy as I'm certain Francie and Martin are at this moment."

"There was something else too." Sally knew now why Francie had always confided in her grandfather. There was something about old Sam's sympathetic interest which inspired the giving of confidences, the seeking after advice and assurance. "My best friend, the girl I've nursed alongside all the time I've been in the profession, became engaged today," she said slowly. "She's to marry one of the doctors from the General. When he leaves there he hopes to join his father's practice . . . they'll have a cosy house, a well-established home-life, a ready-made background . . ."

"But that wouldn't be your life, Sally," Sam answered firmly. "It just isn't *you*, is it?" He demanded an honest answer as the blue eyes fixed their penetrating gaze on Sally's sherry-brown ones.

"No," Sally answered, but slowly, "at least, not just at present," she admitted. "I may come to envy her, in time."

"Everything changes," Sam observed. "Each day is another new page, its deeds unwritten, its characters unmet. Don't give in, Sally," he advised suddenly. "Don't ever be tempted to take second-rate living any more than you were content to take a good love, but one you couldn't return, in place of the real thing, felt equally by both. Give life a chance, girl," he counselled. "Things have a way of working themselves out, if you let them."

It seemed so easy to talk to him, so easy to mention things she would normally have not mentioned to anyone, that, quite without realising how much of her own anxiety she was revealing, she asked:

"You said Mr. Palmer had . . . said he wanted a number of extra pieces of equipment for the hospital. Is there . . . any hope he'll be getting them?"

Sam gave her a quick glance which seemed to read beneath the apparent casualness of the question, so that Sally hastily amended her remarks.

"I only asked, because I'll be back there soon," she said in some confusion, "and I'll probably be working with Mr. Palmer on one case or another. It's always good to know we have what's needed to cope with any emergency which may arise.

"He'll get all he said he would like to have," Sam said briefly, "and more. The General's a wonderful hospital, and we're lucky in Barcaster to have a hospital like it, with a staff such as we have as well. Matron's a treasure, the doctors and nurses are wonderful, and so, too, are the people who aren't employed in either capacity but who help to keep the wheels of the whole place turning. We must never forget we can't do without them, no matter how humble their jobs may seem. But," he was watching Sally shrewdly as he went on, "in Mr. Palmer we have the finest surgeon we could find anywhere. We're indeed lucky to have him with us."

"We are," Sally said with a fervour which did not escape the old gentleman. Abruptly he turned and looked directly into her eyes as though daring her to attempt to prevaricate.

"It's Curtis, isn't it?" he said softly, compelling her to meet his gaze. "Curtis Palmer is the reason for your not being able to love Mike Amberton . . . or any other man."

"Yes." Sally felt the word had been dragged from her, and yet in some strange way it was a relief to have it said. "He doesn't know," she said sadly. "He doesn't see me, only as a nurse, as one of the nurses at the General, the way he sees everyone, either as a nurse of our hospital or a patient . . ."

"Dedicated, that's the word," Sam announced, leaning back and beginning to refill his pipe. "He's the type who needs a woman to look after him. His mother's done a very good job so far, but she won't always be there. When she's gone he'll know just how much he owes to her, help and encouragement included. A fine family," he went on. He appeared to be lost in his own thoughts, and

his eyes held a faraway look as though he had forgotten
Sally's presence. It was something of a shock to the girl
when there was a tap on the door and Sam rose, beaming.

"That'll be Ned," he said simply. "I haven't driven
myself at night for years, and I thought it better not to
break the habit. I've asked him to drive you to your
Copper Bowl rendezvous and to leave you there. The
place closes at midnight or just after. Ned can come back
for you then. Go and meet your friends, Sally," he
advised, pressing something into her hand. "Give them a
celebration toast with this little bonus. You've earned it.
My girl would never have had the confidence she has
now in a thousand years if she hadn't made a friend of
you. Don't forget," he called after her as she went to the
door which Ned had opened for her and where he now
stood waiting, "tomorrow is another day, and there's
always someone who cares where you are, what you're
doing and how you are feeling. Right now I want you to
forget all your worries. Go and help your friends
celebrate, and when you come back to Queen's Close,
who knows, you may have found a different outlook as a
result of your extended day off!"

He cut short her thanks and hustled her from the room,
his eyes bright and twinkling, so that, for a moment, she
suspected him of having some sort of secret which concerned herself.

'Don't be an ass, Sally,' she cautioned herself as Ned
helped her into the estate car and started off for Barcaster. 'Just because he's pleased that his beloved granddaughter is happy it doesn't mean he's any more interested in you than he was. He's just grateful, as the whole
family is, as they've been all the time.'

She settled down to enjoy the short ride into town, and
as they sped past the place where Mrs. Palmer's mini had
crashed through the hedge, Sally had a mental picture of
the older woman's face, the shock, the pain still visible,
but also the relief that Sally was there.

'She said he talked a lot about me,' Sally remembered.
'But I mustn't read anything into that. It's only natural,
when I've been nursing Francie all this time.'

"Here we are, Nurse." Ned was holding open the door of the estate car outside the brightly illuminated frontage of the Copper Bowl. "And if I'm not greatly mistaken that looks like the friend who's been to Queen's Close to see you so many times. There, with a gentleman at the small table in the far corner."

Sally looked where he pointed. Betty and Pete were sitting, heads very close together, apparently lost in themselves and their own concerns, so that she decided not to interrupt them.

"I think——" she was beginning, when Betty looked up and saw her, and the next minute both of them were waving, gaily inviting her inside to sit at their table.

"They might have been expecting you, Nurse," was Ned's comment. "I'll be back for you, like the boss said, unless I get countermanding orders." He grinned. "Enjoy yourself." And then he was gone.

"Coffee?" Betty invited as Sally sat down beside her. "Sorry we can't splash any more, but we've run out of funds until pay-day."

"This is on me, or rather on Sam Bodman." Sally took out the crumpled paper Sam had pressed into her hand and saw, instead of the one-pound note she had expected to find there and yet been embarrassed to receive, a five-pound note. She stared at it as though she had never seen one before, and for a moment anger flared in her and then died down. Sam would not have intended to embarrass her. He wanted her to know how grateful he and his family were for all she had done for Francie, and to him the note would not mean any more than sixpence in a collecting box would mean to Sally. "He told me to finish my day off up to midnight and to come and help you celebrate," she said a little limply. "You take it, Pete. Get what you think best."

Pete trotted off happily to the bar and left the two friends alone for a moment. Sally stripped off her gloves and looked into her friend's shining eyes.

"Was it a good film, pet?" she asked teasingly. "Or didn't you notice?"

"Not particularly . . . I mean . . . I didn't notice." Betty laughed and blushed a little. "We were . . . otherwise engaged," she admitted. "But something happened which we *did* notice," she chattered on in her usual fashion. "What happened when you got to Queen's Close?" she demanded. "Tell me that first, then I'll tell you my bit."

Crisply, briefly, Sally related what had happened, how she and Mike had finally severed their close association, how Curtis had arrived at Queen's Close just before she went up to her room. She touched but lightly on the restless, unhappy feeling that had been hers after Mike had gone, and went on to tell Betty of the scene by the pool and of what Sam had told her on her return to the house.

"Imagine it being him all the time," Betty interrupted, "and it doesn't sound as though even Francie knew what he had done until after he'd done it and the thing was in print for everyone to read. He sounds quite a formidable old gentleman," she commented. "No wonder he's made more than one fortune. I'd rather have him on my side in an argument. Do go on."

"There isn't much more to tell," Sally said. She told how Curtis had driven away, but she did not tell Betty how she had so far forgotten herself as to ask whether or not the General would get the equipment Curtis had said he needed.

"We talked, and he said my day off wasn't ended yet," she concluded, "then he asked me if there was anywhere we all usually met, so I told him about the Copper Bowl and he sent for Ned—he works for the family—and had me driven down here. Ned's coming back for me just before closing time." She accepted a cigarette and a light from Betty just as Pete returned with their drinks. "Now tell me what happened that you did notice," she ended, waiting.

"It was halfway through the big picture," Betty told her. "Suddenly they interruped the programme . . . you know the way they do if there's a message for someone? They sort of chalk a notice and flash it on to the screen. Well, they wrote that someone had been taken seriously ill and asked if there was a doctor in the audience. Pete went out, but someone else was there before him. Curtis Palmer. We thought we'd seen him, sitting by himself, apparently not looking at the screen, but at any rate the message must have registered. Anyhow"—her eyes twinkled suddenly—"before he'd done more than register surprise and comment on what should be done for the man who'd been taken ill—he had a coronary—he asked Pete if *you* were with us!"

"But he knew I wasn't," Sally protested. "He must have seen me, when he drove up to Queen's Close."

"Seen you?" Betty shot out the question, and Sally felt the betraying colour rush to her cheeks.

"Mike . . . kind of . . . kissed me goodbye," she said softly. "It didn't mean anything."

"Not to *you*," Pete said gently, "but it did to Mike." He smiled at her quickly, reassuringly, as he saw the instant contrite look which came into her eyes. "It isn't your fault, Sally," he said quickly. "We can't love people to order, or even because we want to or feel that we should. And Mike's too grand a person to be put off with pretence, however well meant."

"That's what I feel." Sally was glad he understood. She had felt no one would ever know how badly she had felt about hurting Mike, about not giving him the answer he wanted. "I hope . . . when he starts his new job that he'll find someone else," she said sincerely, "someone he'll grow to love and who'll love him the same way."

"But he'll never forget you, Sally," Pete told her seriously. "I don't believe anyone ever forgets their first love. Only a few are lucky enough to love once, and that for ever. Betty"—he gave his fiancée a quick, warm smile which held all the love he had for her in its depths—"told me she was frantically in love with the path. chap before I came here. When she met me she knew she'd been just hero-worshipping, and she was glad he'd never noticed her, but she'll never forget him, and when I fall short in any way she'll draw comparisons, and I shall always be the loser, but I studied enough psycho to know it doesn't mean a thing, and I'll be glad she kept her dream image."

Sally smiled, but made no comment, and after a moment Pete refilled their glasses and went on talking, almost as much to himself as to the girls.

"It's the same thing for me," he said slowly. "When I was at medical school I idolised a girl—Lorna, her name was—and she didn't see anyone there except the profs. She was dedicated from the word go. She wanted to do mission work. That was her sole reason for wanting to qualify. She wanted to help the suffering millions who hadn't the opportunities of being helped that we have in this country. She's still going her one direct way to her goal, and I know now she'd have taken more notice of me if I'd been some obscure bug instead of a fellow student . . . but she did me good." He grinned at Betty, who grinned back, understanding him. "She taught me to idolise my women, but until I met Betty I never found another one I didn't find myself continually comparing with Lorna. Betty's so different. She has all the appeal Lorna had without being aloof. Lorna knew that one has to be . . . it's a hackneyed word, but there isn't another . . . dedicated, unselfish, self-giving all the time in our job, but Betty knows there's a limit to what a man can do, what his body and mind can take. Lorna didn't acknowledge such limits. But sometimes I shall compare Betty with her—to Betty's disadvantage, until I stop to think how difficult it would have been to *live* with Lorna, and then, although I shall never forget her and shall always be grateful to her, I shall be glad I married Betty . . . and that she loves me."

"It isn't the same thing at all." Sally shook her head, dismissing the idea. "Mike is a journalist, a newspaper man . . ."

"And you're a nurse," Pete said swiftly. "It's just the same, Sally. It wouldn't have worked. It was fine for a friendship, but it wouldn't have worked in any closer relationship, believe me. Mike is the kind of person to whom—because it has to be—the story, the news, is more important than the persons involved, whether the story be simple or tragic. You are, you have to be, a person to whom the personal angle means so much.

Mike lives in a frenzied rush of deadlines. You can undertake caring for someone . . . one case . . . one story . . . over a period of months. Mike lives in a world so different from yours that, sooner or later, there would have been not one but many clashes. You'd see things from such different angles, and you're both devoted to your own fields. No"—he toasted her silently as he drank—"let Mike find a girl such as you said Sam Bodman told you about. They'll probably go round the world together or something, earning their living as they go, reporting back all the things they have seen and done, all the tragic and comic happenings they encounter, but if you had been the one to accompany him you'd have been halted at the first batch of kids suffering from malnutrition, the first victims of any epidemic, your first sight of a leper colony . . . anything and anyone who'd have excited the nursing spirit in you and who would mean just another story—however compassionate they felt—to Mike and this unknown girl reporter you mentioned." Pete cleared his throat and smiled at her. "Which is taking me off my point," he went on. "Mike will never forget you, just as you will never forget him, even though you don't love him . . . not in that sense of the word 'love'. But you've each gained something from that friendship. Now"—the grin was back—"don't spend your time regretting and being sorry for Mike. Be glad, instead, that you both have your memories of the happy times you have had together and that you had the sense not to let it go beyond those limits so that one day you'd both have been sorry."

"You don't think I was . . . am . . . wrong, then, Pete?" Sally asked seriously. "You don't think I should have . . . tried?"

"No." There was no doubt about Pete's answer. "You did the wise thing, the right and sensible thing. You made a clean break without either of you being too badly hurt and while you still had your memories of happiness. It's better, in such a case, to cut your losses, as it were. At the most it means you've each spent time with the other when you might have been out and about looking for someone else. But you may not have found them yet, anyway. And in the meantime you've both gained experience and learned a great deal. You see," he was suddenly so grave that Sally realised now he had been talking with the definite purpose of making her feel better and not, as she had suspected, simply wanting to 'hold the floor', expound his own theories, "when Mike was in the General last year with that bout of appendicitis I saw a great deal of him. We talked a lot together. He was friendly with you and you and Betty were inseparable, so I made a point of cultivating his acquaintance."

"And?" Sally prompted as he was silent.

"Mike never believed you would ever love him," Pete said simply. "He accepted his dismissal before he even proposed. He's known all the time that it would never come to anything, and yet, in case he was wrong, I suppose . . . I'll never know, it's one of the queer things about human beings . . . he was prepared to go on stringing along with you until you finally told him yourself. Now you've done that, he'll be free, free as he never could have been while you were willing to go out with him, accompany him here and there, on work or pleasure bent . . . he'd have kept on proposing until you were both due to retire, and that would have been the waste of two good lives," he ended solemnly.

"And as it is," Sally observed slowly, "there's a chance that he may meet someone else, either this girl Sam spoke of or another one, and find what he wants."

"A very good chance, I'd say," Pete remarked seriously, "and so will you, Sally. Some day."

Across the table Betty flashed him a warning glance, but Pete seemed unaware of it. He was looking towards the door, and Sally's glance followed his own. Mike was coming in, big, broad-shouldered, his clothes and hair as usual in some disorder, but the same eager look on his face which characterised him so well. He saw their small party and grinned, waving and making his way over to them without a trace of embarrassment or rancour in his expressive face. Suddenly Sally knew they could meet and talk, and part without any feeling of constraint, because Mike was Mike, and, as Pete had just said, he had accepted her dismissal, but it would make no difference to the true friendship they would always have, one for the other.

CHAPTER NINETEEN

SALLY had thought she would be embarrassed when next she met Mike, but there was no embarrassment in his greeting, no avoidance of her eyes, nothing but the friendly smile to which she was so accustomed. He showed no sign of dejection, none of the miserable air she had dreaded to see, and indeed as he sat down beside Pete he looked as happy as at any time she had ever seen him.

'Pete was right,' Sally told herself, and in spite of the fact that she was glad Mike wasn't miserable, she was human enough to feel a little pang and to wonder if, after all, his protests of love had been sincere, since he had evidently accepted his final dismissal so lightly. His first words as he joined their group soon told her the truth. His words of love had indeed been sincere, but, as Pete had already pointed out to her, he had never believed anything would come of his devotion, and he was not, therefore, as downcast as he might have been. He was putting the best face possible on things, and, being Mike, it was a very good face.

"It's nearly time for closing the bar," he began, "and the drinks are on me." He grinned round at the other three. "I know Betty and Pete have had their celebration, now you can all join in mine and wish me well. I'm leaving Barcaster, first thing in the morning."

"Leaving?" Betty looked from Mike to Sally and back to Mike again. "Don't be too hasty," she was beginning, when Mike gave a shout of laughter, summoned a passing waiter and gave their orders before offering any explanation.

"I'm not being hasty," he said quietly. "I'm being

hustled. I was back at the office, working on some stuff for tomorrow's edition. Normally only the night editor's phone is connected at this time, and there's nobody on the switchboard. I don't know how he did it, but Sam Bodman got through to *me*. Len Fearnley, the editor of our paper at Milcaster, is retiring. He says he wants to go at once . . . Sam's offered me the job and I've from now to the end of the week to work with Len and see how he's running things, but"—and Sally saw that his eyes were alight with enthusiasm and a thousand ideas were already pelting their way though his active brain—"if I want to make any changes I have a free rein, providing I let Sam Bodman know first what I want to do."

"That's wonderful." Sally found her tongue and looked directly at him, meaning every word sincerely. "You always wanted to make changes in Martin Howbury's suggestions and ideas," she remembered. "Now you can try out your own ideas and see for yourself how they go. I'm glad for you, Mike," she said sincerely, "and I know you'll make it one of the best papers in the provinces."

"It's not such a bad one as it is." Mike was honest and he met her glance squarely. "It's a fine paper, but it could be better, and it's going to be from now on. It's what I needed . . . just at this moment," he said quietly. "I don't know how old Sam knew, but he must have had an idea I've nothing to keep me in Barcaster now, and the Milcaster paper has a much bigger circulation."

"I'm glad," Sally told him again, her eyes shining now she knew he would not brood, would not be walking about Barcaster seeing her in so many of the places where they had spent so much time together. "I've just been thinking," she ended, startling them all, "about leaving the General as soon as I can and applying for something different. Maybe overseas work. I've done my tropical training . . ."

"I don't like it," Betty announced suddenly, her mouth taking on the mutinous lines Sally knew so well. "All this change . . . Pete and I are making a change, yes, but it's not the same thing. We're staying on where we are for a time, even after we're married. Then we shan't move far away. Barcaster will still be the centre of our little world, Barcaster and the people in and around it."

"You're in a rut, Betty." Mike grinned at her. "Milcaster isn't the end of the world, you know. It's sort of the mother town to the smaller ones in this area. It's simply that I've got a promotion I might have been waiting for years for in Barcaster, maybe for the rest of my life, and Sally——"

What he was going to say about her Sally never learned, for just then the proprietor of the Copper Bowl hurried over to their table with the important, bustling air he always wore when one or another of Mike's 'contacts' telephoned there with news of some interest from the point of view of the Press.

"Excuse me," he began, glancing round at them all, "but your friend Mentor has telephoned. There's an explosion and a fire at the new works down Chapel Avenue. It started in the chemical department——"

Before he could complete his sentence there was the sound of the fire engine racing along the main street, bells clanging, siren wailing, and a second or so later it raced past the entrance of the Copper Bowl.

"Two ambulances!" Pete and Mike were both on their feet, staring over the heads of the assembled diners through the huge plate-glass window with its shrouding drapes. "Come on, Betty. We'd better get back. It's some sort of chemical factory. There may be only one, there may be dozens of casualties. I don't know much about the place, but I know it's something to do with radiation . . . all the guards and so forth . . ."

"Be seeing you, love." Betty grabbed her handbag, reached over and gave Sally a quick and totally unexpected kiss on her cheek and paused to whisper. "Don't go making any decisions until we've had a talk about it, will you?" she begged. "And in any case, don't you *dare* go and live away until after our wedding. I want you to be my bridesmaid. We always planned it, remember? Whichever one of us married first."

"I remember," Sally said, and gave her friend a little push. Pete had been outside and started his car and now reappeared in the doorway, anxiously looking for his fiancée. "See you," Sally said, but she felt a quick, sharp stab of envy as Betty bustled off, not knowing yet what was required of them, but knowing they would be needed.

"Coming?" For a moment Sally did not think she had heard aright, then she looked up into Mike's eager face. He was anxious to be on the scene, to get his report first hand and quickly, and up to tonight she would have been ready to go with him, if she could not go back to the hospital. Now she knew she must refuse.

"I'd like to." Honesty compelled that admission from her. "I've expected something like this ever since they started the blessed factory, but I promised I'd wait here for Ned."

"Leave a message at the desk," Mike urged. "Bill won't close the Copper Bowl on time tonight, there'll be too many late-night customers. Look at the people pouring out now, just to see what's happened, what's going on. Mr. Bodman'll understand. He knows enough about newspapers to see the value in this."

"But I'm a nurse," Sally began to protest, but she was weakening and Mike knew it. "And I'm supposed to be at the Bodmans'," she said with a sudden, sharp bitterness, "not at the General, where I might be of some help."

"Reason it out afterwards, Sally," Mike urged, "but come with me *now*. Ned'll wait."

It seemed the most natural thing in the world for Sally to obey him. They left a message at the desk, and Bill, owner of the restaurant, promised to look after Ned when he arrived until they returned. Then they were off, Mike's foot on the accelerator when and where he could, hurrying through the crowds which, as always, had gathered when there was anything out of the ordinary happening.

A third ambulance came racing down the road, lights flashing, bell shrilling. Sally bit her lips.

"I . . . there'll be burns," she said quietly, scarcely aware of Mike, thinking only of how, had she still been at the General, she might have been called in to help.

Mike did not answer. All his concentration was on driving, and in a short space of time they were turning into Chapel Avenue and slowly edging their way to where they could see the fire lighting the night sky. Of the fire engine and the ambulances there was no sign. It was evident they had been admitted through the big gates, where a number of policemen stood on guard. Mike braked the car, swung himself out of it brandishing his press card and took a hold of Sally's arm, but they were halted at the gates by a fresh-faced youthful constable.

"Your card, please, miss?" he spoke to Sally, and even Mike's brief "She's with me," was of no use this time. "Sorry, miss," the constable said, and Sally was left outside as Mike was permitted to pass into the factory yard, where a few other pressmen like himself were being prevented from going further by more policemen.

Sally hung about a little while, waiting with those who had congregated out of curiosity. By and by an ambulance was allowed through the gates and made its way through the crowds, heading, Sally knew, for the General. She recognised the driver at the wheel; it was Bob Mentor, the young man who so often telephoned Mike when disaster hit anywhere in the town or its locality.

"Doesn't seem much anyone can do." A man close to Sally spoke to no one in particular, but seeing Sally's interested glance, addressed himself to her. "I've worked here ever since it opened," he stated, "and I've expected this. Not that what the precautions aren't good; they are. But there's always someone doesn't take what precautions are provided. Always someone who doesn't care."

Someone else had said something almost like that but not quite, to her, not so long ago. Sally frowned, trying to remember. Then the frown cleared. Sam Bodman had said "there's always someone who cares . . ." There was no connection, it just struck her how strange that Sam should be so convinced there was "someone who cared" and this stranger equally convinced there were those who didn't care.

"Fire engine's coming back now," the man announced. "Can't have been much or they'd have had the big engines over from Milcaster. Look, they've finished."

Sally did not answer. The man sounded disappointed,

but that, she told herself, was absurd. He was probably anticipating some extra excitement and felt cheated because it was all over so quickly, but Sally was only relieved that there were not more people injured. She watched keenly as the other two ambulances followed the fire engine from the inner yard, then she turned to the man who appeared to be better informed than anyone else around.

"Have there been many people injured, do you know?" she asked quietly.

"Six, I think." The man eyed her for a moment, then said suddenly, "You work at the hospital, don't you? I remember seeing you when my little girl was ill last year."

"Yes." Sally did not remember him, but it was not necessary to say so. There was a new respect in his attitude now, as though he could picture her in uniform, and she had thereby gained added status. "I'm working away from the General just now," she said quickly, "but I'll soon be back there. I wondered ..."

"Two men were badly burned. Chap in the first ambulance had his arm injured. They do say it'll have to be amputated, but I don't know," the man said briefly. "You folks do such wonderful things nowadays. Put new insides into people, or so I've read. Not much you can't do, is there? Guess it won't take long to patch that little lot up ... make 'em as good as new. It must be wonderful to have a job like yours, Nurse. Sort of satisfying ..."

Sally stared at him a moment, then she smiled. Suddenly it was as though a weight had been lifted from her heart. Curtis was content to do just that ... a satisfying job of helping people, of restoring them to health and new life, and that was what she must be ... satisfied and content to help, alongside him, not 'wishing for the moon', being content to serve.

"It is," she told the stranger. "Very wonderful." Then, with a murmured "Excuse me," she went off to find Mike.

He was with a small knot of workers, just inside the gates, and from past experience Sally knew he would now be busily engaged in getting eye-witness accounts of the accident. Mike, with the permission of his employers, made a useful addition to his income by news paragraphs, and, had he but known it, it was his unerring sense of a story which had, long ago, attracted him to Sam Bodman's notice. He looked up and gestured with his pencil as he saw Sally.

"All over but the shouting," he said quickly. "I'm just getting a few eye-witness notes and observations. Shouldn't take long. Find yourself a corner somewhere."

How often he had said those same words to her on many such an occasion, and how often she had waited! This time she smiled, shook her head and turned away.

"I'm going back to wait for Ned, Mike," she told him over her shoulder. "He should be here about now. In the morning I'm going to telephone Matron and ask to be taken back to the General . . . tomorrow, if possible."

"You do that." Mike's pencil was flying, his eyes were hidden as he kept his glance firmly on his note-pad. He turned to the man he was interviewing. "What happened then?" he demanded, and as the man gathered together his recollections to reply, Mike looked up and grinned at Sally. "Ring me," he said briefly, "later . . . will you?"

Sally nodded and moved away. Mike's pencil was already busy again. He had not forgotten her, he would never do that, but what Pete had said was true. The story came first for Mike, it always would, before personal loss or gain, joy or sorrow, and, as she made her way carefully through the thinning crowds, Sally was glad that for Mike this was so. Now she could go ahead and plan her own life in an entirely different way, dedicating it to the service of others, as she had already done, but with this difference . . . now her dedication would be more heart-whole than ever, since she had set Mike free and she would model herself as far as she could on Curtis Palmer, thinking not whether she would be happy, but how much more could she serve.

She was still basking in this rather satisfying glow of self-sacrifice as she returned to the Copper Bowl. The lights had been dimmed, the tables cleared, the chairs stacked in deference to the police issue of licence, but the door was open and Bill stood on the threshold. He moved inside as he saw Sally approach.

"Ned hasn't arrived yet, miss," he greeted her, holding the door open and motioning Sally to precede him inside. "But Mr. Bodman—Mr. Bodman senior—telephoned a little while ago and said you were to wait until someone came for you. He said it wouldn't be Ned, but that you'd recognise the person. He said they'd probably be about half an hour, and that you were to wait." He eyed her for a moment then added: "We live here, my wife and family and myself, miss. I told Mr. Bodman I'd have to close the restaurant, but that I'd invite you to take coffee with us ... if you don't mind?"

"I'd love it," Sally told him solemnly. "It's most kind of you to take all this trouble. I could get a taxi, I suppose ..."

"Mr. Bodman particularly asked that you should wait," Bill informed her. "I said it would be all right, and, believe me," his tone was sober and serious, "when Mr. Bodman asks you to do something, then there's usually a pretty good reason for doing it."

"You know him well, then?" Sally went through the door he indicated and found herself in a cosy room where a pleasant-faced woman bustled about bringing freshly made coffee and hot rolls.

"He lent me the money to start this business," Bill said quietly. "When I came back, after the war, and that's some years ago now, I felt I'd nothing to live for. My folks were all gone. They lived on the south coast. A buzz-bomb took what was left of my family. I didn't want to make a fresh start. I'd been a cook in the Forces. I did some fancy dishes here for one of his dinners, more because I needed to eat that night myself than for any other reason. He talked to me afterwards, said how much he'd enjoyed what I'd made and asked me if I'd any plans. I hadn't any, as I've told you. Didn't seem to care about making any, but Mr. Bodman said, very sternly, as I thought then, that *he* cared ... that he cared about everybody, but he could only help when he knew of a need."

Bill pushed the huge cup of hot coffee towards her and handed her the cream and sugar, a strange smile creasing his rather tired face.

"I don't know now how it came about," he said slowly, rubbing his jaw in a reflective manner as though he were trying to puzzle something out, "but somehow he made me feel he really *did* care . . . and it did something for me. I began to feel that if a stranger cared that I didn't waste my life it was up to me not to waste it, and when he offered me the chance to take this place and make something of it, well, I accepted."

"You've done well." Sally felt something was expected of her, but Bill merely nodded, smiling across at his wife.

"The place is O.K.," he said briefly. "It's a good little business now, and folks come from all over for special dinners, lunches, suppers and what-have-you, but the more important thing is that I've got a life too. I've a wife I met through the business, I've two fine children who'll grow up and inherit it if they want to, and I'm not in the least like the same chap who came home to find he didn't think there was anything left to live for, and it's all due to old Sam Bodman . . ."

"And a great deal to yourself and your own endeavour," Sally put in.

Bill nodded.

"There's that, too," he agreed, "but I'd never have found it out for myself. 'There's always someone who cares,' was what he said to me, and I kept on believing it . . . now there's a family who care, as well as Mr. Bodman, and he's proud I justified his belief in me, so when he says to ask you to wait, why, that's what I did. And what I'd do if I were you, miss." He was suddenly serious again, advising her. "That's what I'd do if I were you."

"Then I will," Sally said, settling down and helping herself to a roll and butter. "I'll wait for my escort, however long he is in arriving."

CHAPTER TWENTY

THE hands of the clock had crept round a further thirty minutes or more when there came a premonitory rapping on the door of the Copper Bowl. Bill, who had been happily telling Sally of some of his wartime experiences, jumped to his feet and went from the cosy little living-room, calling over his shoulder.

"That'll be whoever it is coming to fetch you, Nurse. I'll get your coat as I come through. Don't hurry, in case it's someone else."

Sally looked up as he returned, hearing him speaking to someone, but she felt herself go suddenly white as, close on his heels into the little room, Curtis appeared, seeming to tower above Bill.

"Is . . . something wrong?" she began nervously. "Ned . . . isn't hurt? There hasn't been *another* accident?"

"Ned's perfectly all right, so far as I know," Curtis said quietly after greeting Bill's wife. "I want you to come with me, Sally. It's an emergency," he added, as though on an afterthought.

"I can't." She was appalled. *He* was asking for her help and she was not in a position to give it. She was still under orders, Matron's orders, working at the Bodman house, yes, but still part of the staff of the General.

"Why not?" There was the note she had heard in his voice so often in the General, the note which said he was displeased, that he didn't intend to be thwarted.

"I'm waiting for someone to take me back to Queen's Close," she explained. "I'm still supposed to be looking after Francesca Bodman, you know."

"I know." A brief smile touched his lips and was gone so quickly that she could not be sure it had ever been there at all. "Francie is all right," he announced as if the matter were of no consequence, "and Mr. Bodman telephoned me . . . I telephoned Matron, so"—the smile was back in full now—"all honour is satisfied. You're to come with me—if you will, Sally—and both Mr. Bodman *and* Matron know where you are."

There was something different about him, something on which she could not put her finger, but she moved to take her coat.

"An emergency, you said?" she asked quietly. "Surely the General would have been . . ." and then bit her lip. She had taken to thinking of him as a *person* so much and so often of late she was forgetting it was not her place to question his statements, his orders. He did not appear to have noticed the slip, but nodded gravely, helping her on with her coat, which suddenly seemed difficult to manage alone.

"The General would hardly have been the place for what I'm thinking of," he said enigmatically. "Are you ready?"

Sally nodded, said goodnight to Bill and his wife, thanking them for their hospitality, promising to come again, and not always as a customer, but as a friend. Then Curtis had taken her by the elbow and was guiding her from the restaurant with its subdued lighting so dim in these non-opening hours as to be confusing, and down the steps and to his car. He helped her in and closed the door, then reached into the back and took up a folded travelling rug, leaning in to tuck it carefully about her.

"You'll need that," he said gently. "The evening air gets chilly."

Sally felt completely mystified as he walked round the car and took his place beside her in the driver's seat. He lifted a hand in farewell salute to Bill, then the car moved swiftly and silently away, heading in the direction of the Bodmans', it was true, but turning off a little way before the place in the road where his mother's mini had gone through the hedge. Sally shivered, remembering, and then, with a glance at his set profile, ventured a question.

"How is your mother?" she asked quietly. "I ought to have asked as soon as I saw you, but I didn't expect you. I'm sorry."

"I know." Curtis's voice was suddenly very gentle and the car slowed a little as he answered. "Mother is very well, considering the shock she received," he told her. "I took her home this evening. She was a little like Mrs. Bodman would have been in like circumstances . . . she didn't like the rules and what-have-you at the General, although she knew perfectly well they were for her own good and that of the other patients. She wanted to be home, there was no reason why she shouldn't go, so I took her."

"I'm glad," Sally said, and meant it, but she was unprepared for what came next.

"She'd like you to come and see her, Sally," Curtis told her. "You will, won't you?"

"I—of course," Sally answered. "I said I would. As soon as she has recovered a little."

"I think," Curtis said slowly, "you could . . . assist in that recovery, Sally. Just as you assisted in Francie's. You have a marvellous restorative effect upon people. Did you know that?"

She noticed then that he had stopped the car, that they were in a small country road which had led off the main road and was evidently the entrance to some private drive. He was behaving so strangely that suddenly she wondered what this was all about. She was not afraid, but there was a mounting sense of something pounding in her veins and she was suddenly fearful that this might not mean what she was just beginning to hope it might mean. She asked quickly: "Where are we? Where are we going? Where is this emergency?"

"Here," Curtis said simply, leaning over and suddenly taking both her hands in his strong but gentle ones. "Right here," he reiterated. "I'm the . . . emergency."

"You!" Sally stared at him, wondering if this were all some dreadful joke, if in some way he was making fun of her, but he held her hands tightly when she would have freed them, and suddenly his face was very close to her own.

"I am," he said slowly, impressing the words with weight. "Oh, Sally, you don't know what you've done to me, what you mean to me. When I saw Mike Amberton kissing you tonight, I felt then it was the end of everything I'd hoped for, dreamed about. Up to then I'd had a faint hope . . . Mother said he was just a friend . . . but then . . ."

"He was . . . kissing me goodbye," Sally told him. "He's going away."

"I know that . . . *now*," Curtis answered. "I didn't . . . then."

"And . . . now?" Sally asked him, a little smile playing round the corners of her mouth as his arms came round her and his face even closer. "What do you think now?"

"Mr. Bodman told me," Curtis said gently, gravely. "He told me a number of things which I should have seen for myself. He told me he had been the one to see . . . what's her name? Mavis. It was all his doing, but he'd got what he wanted, he'd gained Francie's happiness. He told me that you thought . . . that the equipment mattered. It does, but not as much as you matter, and he'll give it anyway. He told me Mike was going away and that he was thrilled with his new job. He told me that . . . you love me . . . and I shan't believe that until you tell me yourself . . . and that you'd be at the Copper Bowl and I could pick you up and take you home as soon as we were through with the poor souls in the explosion tonight. Tell me that he's right again, Sally. Tell me that he knew what he was talking about and that I can drive right on from here . . . this little lane ends in the drive-way of my home . . . and that's were I want to take you *now*. Tell me," he insisted as his arms tightened about her and Sally spoke no word, "just tell me he was right in all this . . . and that it's true, you *do* love me . . . always will."

"I do, and I always will," Sally said as solemnly as if she were giving an oath. Then the little smile she could not repress peeped out again as she gave herself up to his kiss. "And of course he's right . . . how could a Bodman be wrong?" And Curtis, too, was laughing as at long last he folded her in his arms where, he knew now, she would always belong.

Other 'Medical'
Harlequin
Romances
you may enjoy

Over the years when Harlequin Romances have been published, many of our most popular titles have been stories revolving around life and romance in medical fields throughout the world.

An assortment of some of these titles, available through the Harlequin Reader Service, is listed on the back of this page.

Should you wish to obtain any, simply fill out the order coupon below.

Other 'Medical'
Harlequin Romances
you may enjoy . . .

All books are 50c. Please use the handy order coupon.

FREE!

*Harlequin
Romance
Catalogue*

Here is a wonderful opportunity to read many of the Harlequin Romances you may have missed.

The HARLEQUIN ROMANCE CATALOGUE lists hundreds of titles which possibly are no longer available at your local bookseller. To receive your copy, just fill out the coupon below, mail it to us, and we'll rush your catalogue to you!

Following this page you'll find a sampling of a few of the Harlequin Romances listed in the catalogue. Should you wish to order any of these immediately, kindly check the titles desired and mail with coupon.

To: **HARLEQUIN READER SERVICE, Dept. BP,**
M.P.O. Box 707, Niagara Falls, N.Y. 14302
Canadian address: Stratford, Ont., Canada

☐ Please send me the free Harlequin Romance Catalogue.

☐ Please send me the titles checked.

I enclose $＿＿＿＿＿ (No C.O.D.'s), All books are 50c each. To help defray postage and handling costs, please add 25c.

Name ＿＿＿＿＿＿＿＿＿＿＿＿＿＿＿＿＿＿＿＿

Address ＿＿＿＿＿＿＿＿＿＿＿＿＿＿＿＿＿＿＿

City/Town ＿＿＿＿＿＿＿＿＿＿＿＿＿＿＿＿＿

State/Prov. ＿＿＿＿＿＿＿＿＿＿＿ Zip＿＿＿＿＿

Have You Missed Any of These
Harlequin Romances?

All books are 50c.   Please use the handy order coupon.